DARING MR. DARCY

Your new favorite rom-com retelling of
Miss Austen's classic!

Elissa Bennet has jumping to conclusions down to a fine art, and her first impression of Liam Darcy leaves her less than impressed. Liam isn't so easily put off, but is his interest in Elissa real, or a determination to meet his sister's dare?

Because it is a truth universally acknowledged, that a man in charge of a large fortune must be in want of a wife. Or so Liam Darcy's grandma insists, and his sister, Georgia, agrees. But no sweet grandmotherly ultimatum or sassy sister dare can influence Liam to go so far outside his comfort zone as hunt for a woman to marry.

That is until new-to-town Elissa Bennett makes an appearance. Hey, a dare is a dare, right? But Liam's attempts to impress end in disaster, and feisty Elissa is not afraid to say so. Liam Darcy is the last person on earth she'd be tempted to date. Until sparks fly...

Carolyn Miller and Meredith Resce have retold Miss Austen's timeless *Pride and Prejudice* in a laugh-out-loud contemporary rom-com. *Daring Mr Darcy* can be read as a standalone novel, and is perfect for lovers of sweet, clean romance.

DARING MR DARCY

CAROLYN MILLER
MEREDITH RESCE

CHAPTER 1

"*B*ecause, my dear William, it is a truth, universally acknowledged, that a single man in possession of a good fortune must be in want of a wife."

I choke, coffee spluttering everywhere as my grandmother looks at me with those blue eyes that always spelled trouble. Is she insane? The lack of a smile, the non-blinking stare, and use of my full name suggest she might actually be serious. My insides tense, and I straighten from my non-boardroom-approved slouch. "No."

"No?" Her feathery white eyebrows peak, and I'm pitched back fifteen years to when Georgia and I first came to live here and had to learn the ways of a grandparent who, until then, had always possessed something of a mythical element. Olivia Grace Darcy was not someone to trifle with.

I put the coffee mug on the table, place my elbows on my knees and study her, hoping to project the cool that had seen Pemberley Enterprises leapfrog into Forbes' top one hundred new businesses two years ago. "Gran, I love you, but I do *not* want a wife."

She sighs, the sound as soft as a feather, and equally ticklish to my conscience. Was anything harder to deal with than an elderly woman sighing like you're personally responsible for all her disappointments? Except, maybe, when it's from the woman who'd basically raised you when a drunk driver cut your family in half fifteen years ago. "William—"

Uh oh. She has her warning voice on.

"I'm getting old, and this ranch needs a future."

"Come on, Gran. You're gonna live forever." She had to. "We're all going to be living here for years."

Gran's eyes laser me into silence, and I'm suddenly aware that for all her steel, she is over eighty, and one day wouldn't be around. A new tension grips my gut. "Gran, are you sick? You need to tell me if you are. You know Georgia will take it better hearing it from me than—"

"I'm not sick. Except—"

Except what? My chest clenches.

"Except I'm sick with worry about what will happen to you both when I'm gone."

The steel bands across my chest clank free at the unsatisfactory answer, the complaint one I've heard dozens of times since I'd turned thirty. But come on. "This isn't the 1950s, Gran. I've got plenty of time to settle down."

"Your father was married and had two children by thirty."

Yeah, but my dad hadn't cracked the Forbes rich list by then, either.

My backside starts buzzing, and I draw my phone from my back pocket and place it on the smoked-glass coffee table, where it begins a twisted dance toward Georgia's white-iced gingerbread house remains. Nope. Not gonna answer. My gaze itches to find out who'd be calling on Christmas Day, and I have to grip my hands together to stop my trigger-ready fingers from playing guess,who. But it didn't stop my brain. Had the Japanese deal fallen through? Had the Austrian merger found a new hiccup? Was there a problem in Burundi?

Gran frowns, as if recognizing my mental torment. "You are addicted to that phone, aren't you?"

"No." I hold up both hands, force my gaze to level with hers. "See? Not addicted."

"Please." Another sigh, louder this time. "It's like you are permanently attached to that thing."

"I need it for work, Gran. You know that." I'm trying to be patient. It's not like we haven't had this discussion, oh, sixty times before.

"I know you're a workaholic. It's not healthy."

"I work hard, Gran. Aren't you proud that the company is doing so well?"

"You know I am," she says, her features softening. "But I also want you to be happy."

"I am happy. I *like* working."

"But you're always on edge, and even when you're here it's like you're not really here."

I bite my tongue, not wanting to point out the obvious. Success required focus, not fluffing around having so-called fun.

"I'm just worried about you, dear."

Man. She really went there and pulled out the 'dear' card. Things must be serious.

"I can't remember the last day off you had," she continues.

"Work keeps me busy—"

"Too busy for friends," she interrupts.

"I have friends," I insist.

"Who?" She holds up a ruby ring-encrusted finger. "And don't give me anyone who works with you."

Oh. Uh… "Jackson."

"From next door?"

I nod and settle back in my seat, relieved at finding someone. "He and Caleb said something about getting together at New Year's."

"Did they now?" Her eyes gleam with interest. "And what exactly did they say?"

"Jackson's got some function on." A dinner, maybe. Dinners always offered the two-for-one special of food and business. Get your meal, get your talking done, then get out of there. I hoped it was a dinner, anyway. Probably should've paid more attention to whatever Jackson and Caleb had been talking about the other day.

"Well, perhaps that will work," she murmurs.

Work for what? My eyebrows lift.

"A new year." She nods, as if deciding something. "Very well. William, I want you to promise me something."

"Sure. What is it?" Anything.

"This year, I want you to think about finding a girlfriend."

I cough. Anything—except maybe that.

"Not like that last girl, Cathy someone?"

"Cassandra Bellingham," I correct.

"Hmm. I've never been fond of artificial enhancements, shall we say, even if such things appeal to young men."

My neck burns, and I resist the urge to loosen my collar. Okay, so Cassie's enhancements hadn't exactly been hard to ignore. But it didn't matter how much I insisted I was more interested in her brains than anything else, Gran never believed me.

"No, find someone nice, someone who doesn't care about your money or your family connections."

Yeah, and pigs might soar heavenwards.

"Someone your mother would've loved, who Georgia can see as a sister."

My chest pangs.

"Please, do this for me?"

I shift on the soft leather sofa, reluctance steaming out of every pore.

"Don't scowl at me, my boy. The wind might change, and—"

"Gran, I really think you're being unreasonable."

"No. Unreasonable would be saying I'll change my will and ensure your inheritance goes to the Trinity Lakes Hospital instead of you."

I blink. Nope. My grandmother is still sitting there, looking Angela Lansbury sugar sweet, and not as if she's just dropped an atom-bomb. "You're not serious."

Her lips lift. "I am."

Disbelief pushes out in laughter. "What are they going to do with fifty million dollars?"

"A lot of good, I imagine."

No. I sink back in the cushions, her gaze pinning me like a dancing cobra.

"And while I do believe in supporting our local health system, I would actually like to see you happy and settled."

"Gran, I am happy."

"Really?"

How is it that six letters can skewer my lie?

"You only get one life, William," she says softly. "Make it count and be happy. What have you got to lose by saying yes, anyway?"

What have I got to lose?

Gran's question chases me from the warm comfort of the living room as I punch the phone to find my answer from before. Ben Morrow. The only man in the world who loathed Christmas more than me. No wonder he's happy to call. I'm about to return his call when Georgia walks into the kitchen. My finger hovers over my phone for a microsecond, then I push it back into my pocket. Unlike Gran I know how to withhold a sigh. "Hey, Georgia Grace. Good movie?"

Her green eyes are the sparkliest I've seen in months. "I like a good rom-com."

I nod, like I know what she means. But the last movie I watched was over a year ago, and I've always been more of an action fan than anything involving romance or comedy. Get it done, get on with it, move on, that's my scene. Feelings? Not so much.

But Georgia was all about feelings, and the counsellor had said she needed to feel 'heard,' so I was trying to do better. Be patient, stop to listen, and all that kind of thing.

"You and Gran seemed to be chatting for a while," she says.

I eye her as I grab the last of Brenda's silver-ball-dusted ginger cookies. Our cook has really outdone herself this year. I'm about to take a bite when I remember these are GG's favorites. "You want?" I ask, holding it out to her.

"Sure."

Before I can blink she snatches it from my hand and stuffs it in her mouth, her eyes twinkling with the mischief I see so rarely. Huh. "Looks like someone should've eaten a little more Christmas turkey at lunch."

"Looks like someone is trying to change the subject." She daintily wipes beside her mouth. "So, what were you and Gran talking about for so long?"

"Just things." Like I'm about to tell my little sister anything about my personal life. Not that I've got anything to tell. Anyway, the last time I had, Georgia hadn't exactly held back about her opinion of Cassie and the hundreds of ways she was wrong for me, calling her everything from fake to a gold-digger. She gets that bluntness—and discernment—from my grandmother.

"Uh huh." She eyes me in that annoying little sister way she has, clearly waiting for an answer.

But she'll never be too annoying. Not when she and Gran are the only two remaining members of my family, and the only two people who I'll do anything to protect.

"Gran wants me to go out more," I finally admit.

Her eyebrows rise. "As in...?"

"As in find a girlfriend next year, yes."

She grins, and it's like I'm seeing my sister from two years ago, and an ache blooms across my chest. "But I have to like her, okay? Don't go getting another trashy Cassie."

"That's not nice now, GG."

"Yeah, well, she wasn't. Nice, that is. I'll never forget what she called me."

The radiance drains from her face and I'm already regretting having said things to remind her. If only I'd known just what a mouth my ex had behind those plumped-up lips. "Forget it. It's in the past."

She nods. "And someone new is in your future, right?"

"Gran sure hopes so," I say, wryness edging my tone and my heart.

"I do, too." Georgia rubs her hands together. "So, you're going to?"

"Going to what?"

"Find yourself a girl," she says slowly, like I'm three.

"It's not as easy as that," I warn. "It's not like this town is full of attractive available women."

"He says, like he's never heard of the internet," she murmurs. "Oh, and like he doesn't spend half the year traveling."

"What's the point in finding someone who lives a thousand miles away?"

"I didn't figure you as someone who ever took the easy option, brother dear." Her gaze is innocent, her tilted chin holding a challenge.

I draw in a deep breath of cinnamon and turkey-scented air and slowly release. "You're a brat, you know that?"

Light dances in her eyes as I grab a handful of unshelled walnuts and advance. "You're not going to—"

I pitch one, and as it bounces off her arm I laugh.

She gasps and grabs a handful of green and red M&Ms and pelts them at me. "If only everyone could see you now, Mr. Serious!"

"Mr. Serious?" What was she? Twelve?

She nods. "Everyone believes all you think about is money and making the next deal."

They did?

Maybe my concern shows in my face for she stops her assault, her features softening. "You need to have more fun, Liam. You've been caring for me and Gran for so long it's time you thought about your own needs for a change."

Her comment puts me in mind of what Gran said not so long ago. Yeah, but this single man definitely neither needed nor wanted a girlfriend, let alone a wife, thank you very much.

"I dare you," she says, smirking, knowing dares are my Achilles heel.

Suddenly the prospect of a New Year's Eve dinner seems way too close for comfort.

～

"Elissa's not seeing anyone at the moment." Mum has chosen a lull in the dinner table conversation to make her loud announcement. Truly, could this get any more awkward? I can feel the blood rushing to my face, and a quick look in Jane's direction shows she's embarrassed as well. Mum only opens her mouth to change feet. Apparently, she hasn't finished.

"Shame you only have two sons." Mum indicates the Kennedy boys as if they have been waiting all their life for this brilliant opportunity.

"Mum!" I have to stop this travesty. The delicious Christmas dinner is beginning to revolt in my stomach.

Mum holds her hand up as if it's of no account. "We've lived out in the country for so long, and there are no marriage prospects out there for our girls. I thought Elissa would find someone when she went to Sydney, but..." She shrugs her shoulders.

"This cranberry sauce is delicious." This is the best diversion I can muster.

"We don't usually eat turkey at Christmas." Lydia's observation is less to aid my cause and more a stating of the obvious.

"I remember." Marianne Kennedy is the consummate host and doesn't appear ruffled by my mother's lack of social grace. "We lived in your town for five years and loved eating shrimp and cold ham as a change at Christmas."

"Anyway..." Mum hasn't been derailed and I can tell she's circling back for another approach. "Wouldn't it be funny if our girls matched up with your boys?"

Caleb and Matt are in the room. How they can continue to eat the food on their plate is beyond me. I'm ready to fake a choking fit and have them call an ambulance just to escape the mortification.

"Caleb has a girlfriend, as it happens." James Kennedy is matter-of-fact. When he taught me math in year eight, he was always straight to the point, and never minded if anyone was embarrassed by it. Still, the news of Caleb's girlfriend is a relief. A quick glance in Caleb's direction and he is deeply involved with his roast potatoes. Either he's missed all of Mum's subtle-as-a-brick matchmaking hints or he's decided that concentrating on his food will be the best way to avoid engaging.

"What a shame." Mum has no tact.

"I'm sure Caleb is perfectly happy as he is, Francis." It's about time Dad said something.

"Yes, but our girls aren't getting any younger. I don't want to be too old to enjoy grandchildren."

Shoot me now.

"Well, I wish you luck." Marianne doesn't seem to be too alarmed by the direction of Mum's thoughts. "Now, I've a surprise—for my family at least."

"What surprise?" Matt Kennedy has found his voice, probably glad to focus on another subject other than his status as an eligible bachelor.

"I've tried my hand at making a traditional English Christmas pudding. You remember how we enjoyed it as part of our Australian Christmas adventures?" Marianne is smiling at her son. "Who'd like some?"

And just like that, Marianne was able to lead Mum into the kitchen, thanking her for the kind offer to help serve dessert.

"This is why I envy you," Jane says, leaning in for my ears only.

"Why?"

"Because you have the whole Pacific Ocean between you and Mum."

It sounds harsh, but Jane has summed it up perfectly. I thought moving to Sydney and putting half a continent between us would be enough, but before long, she was talking about moving the whole family away from Booleroo Whim to settle in Sydney to be near me. That was my cue to accept the study exchange to Seattle University. At least Mum had calmed down and stopped talking about uprooting the whole family. But now, here they were—Mum, Dad, Jane, and Lydia—on their once-in-a-lifetime trip to North America to see the sights during their summer holidays. Their friendship with the Kennedys made it the perfect place for all of us to meet for our family's first white Christmas experience right here in Trinity Lakes, east Washington State. A world away from rural South Australia, which would be baking in a summer heat wave at the moment, we are enjoying everything we'd ever seen on a Hallmark movie, including snow.

Thankfully, Dad manages to keep the topic of conversation on everything *but* his unmarried daughters over dessert and coffee. I'm a bit miffed that I had been so tense during dinner. I had wanted to immerse myself in the whole Christmas vibe, it being so different to how we celebrate in Australia. Too late now. I'm lucky to get out of it without a betrothal ceremony over Christmas eggnog.

After another exchange of reminisces, we begin the slow task of thanks and farewells and move to the front hall to grab our coats and scarves. Even the short trek from the house to the car holds a frosty bite none of us are used to.

"Hey, Elissa." Matt Kennedy hasn't said much all evening. What could he want now, just as we are about to leave? "If you and your sisters are interested, there's a New Year's Eve barn dance out at Jackson Reilly's place."

"Barn dance?"

"Music, food, friends, in a barn. You never know, we might be able to aid your mother in her quest to get you a man." He's smiling. Actually smiling. Does he think this is funny?

"Ah, thank you for the invitation. I'll talk to Jane and Lydia and see what they have planned."

"We'll come!" Lydia is standing right behind me, apparently. Typical. In her case, the apple doesn't fall far from the tree when it comes to enthusiastic man-hunting.

"Great. Do you want a ride?"

"Yes, please!"

For goodness sake, Lydia. Could you at least pretend you're not desperate?

"We'll let you know." My tone is firm and even. I will not be rushed into a crazy decision. Lydia always jumps first and thinks later. Actually, she doesn't do much thinking, which is mean for me to say, but if I, as her older sister, can't say it as it is, who can? "We need to check with our folks before committing to anything."

"Sure. Whatever."

"It'll be fun." Lucy Kennedy hasn't said much all evening, either, but she seems nice.

"And it's likely Liam Darcy will be there." And now Caleb has decided to speak.

I want to ask, but decorum prevents me.

"Who's Liam Darcy?" Lydia asks the question that satisfies my curiosity.

"He's the richest, most eligible bachelor in the district," Matt says. "Your mom would love him."

I use all my will power to prevent an eye-roll. Lydia's squeal and wide eyes suggest she's practically gagging at the idea, engaged to him already—in her imagination.

"We'll think about it." This is my best impression of indifference. I will not be steamrolled into another awkward situation where there are ridiculous expectations. Mum's failed attempt to hitch me up with Colin Allsopp meant we didn't talk for two weeks—a record for her, a blessed reprieve for me. They could bait me with all the impressive credentials in the world, but I have standards. Rich is not one of them. Being rich usually implies entitled, couldn't-care-less about the environment or other crucial justice issues, so Liam whatever-his-name-is will just have to look somewhere else. I'm not interested.

Jane is smiling. Oh, dear lord. She's got a dreamy look in her eye. Stop it, Jane. Stop it. You're just playing into Mum's hands.

"It was lovely to meet you." Jane's warmth directed at Matt has connected with him. Please don't let Mum see.

"Yes, thank you for a lovely dinner," I say. "It was a wonderful cultural experience." I am now doing my best to appear congenial and appreciative, and hoping to get out of here before something disastrous happens—like Jane falling in love with an American. What could be worse than a sister living overseas?

"Maybe we'll see you at New Year's Eve?" Matt's glance is hovering more than necessary in Jane's direction.

"Maybe." I cast the sweetest smile I can muster in Matt's direction, all to no avail. He's got his eye on Jane.

CHAPTER 2

*W*hoever originally thought parties were a great idea must've had a secret life as a torturer of introverts. And the fact this New Year's Eve event at the Reilly ranch was definitely not just a simple dinner, but a party *and* a dance, was like I was living my worst nightmare. Everything about Jackson's party felt painful. Music: too loud. People: too many. Food: too salty. And as for dancing...

I shudder. Yeah, I know this makes me sound like an old man, but on a scale of one-to-ten in feeling out of my comfort zone, I'm sitting at a solid ninety-nine. I hate parties. All the yelling over music as you pretend to be interested in people you've never met before, faking smiles as you pretend to have a good time, it's exhausting. Give me cool hard facts and figures and quiet boardrooms any time. The only good thing about tonight is that I've been able to coax Georgia out for the first time in months. Maybe the first time all year. Which seems ironic, considering it's the last opportunity to go out this year, but anyway.

I glance across to where she's huddled in the corner near the three-piece band. Close to the musicians, as always. If she's not off photographing something or playing her guitar then she's always got her headphones clamped to her ears.

Her eyes catch mine and she mouths *Having fun?*

I shake my head, and her smile peeks out, as if she knew I'd say no. This gets me thinking about that Mr. Serious comment from six days ago. I haven't been able to stop thinking about that, actually, even despite the meetings that crammed this past week. And yeah, it might've been part of what brought my busy, non-dancing self out to mingle with neighbors and townsfolk I rarely saw, like I was proving myself as Mr. Fun by being here. I eye-roll myself. Like standing on the edges here was proving them wrong.

"Liam, you made it." Jackson, the host with the most, stretches out a hand that I grip.

I nod to his tomboy sister, Eloise, who smiles then goes and talks with Georgia. Bless her.

"You're not dancing?" Jackson points out the obvious.

"I don't dance," I say firmly. It's better for everyone if my uncoordinated self does not partake.

He grins, and I'm reminded of Maisie, the sweet-natured labradoodle we had growing up, all dark brown eyes and curly hair. "And yet here you are at a barn dance."

My stomach tenses, and I really hope he's not going to say—

"And with more women than men, well, you know it's your civic duty to get on the dance floor."

I sigh, then, conscious I'm now really sounding like an old man—or an old woman—slap a smile on my face. "Sure. Eventually." Like when hell freezes over, maybe. Although, judging from the snow dumps of recent days and the wind chill that chased us on the short drive here, maybe that wasn't too far away.

He seems to take that as good enough, slaps my shoulder and goes to talk to some others, and I'm sorely tempted to leave. Or at least pull out my phone. But no. I promised Georgia I would have a phone-free—and thus, business free—evening, so Mr. Serious is gonna hang around and pretend he's actually Mr. Fun.

Right.

My sister draws closer, and I'm suddenly super thankful she's here. She hasn't danced with anyone either, but she kind of has a protective 'don't mess with me' force field that steers most guys away. Which isn't surprising, considering all she's been through.

"You know, I have to congratulate you," she murmurs.

"For what?"

"I haven't seen you look at your phone once. I didn't know you had it in you."

"Oh ye of little faith."

She chuckles, and the sound is so surprising, so welcome, I'm prepared to forgive her for insisting I come tonight. Her stealth technique, to make sure I came, involved outlining to Gran exactly what tonight's details involved. Details I'd somehow forgotten, but she'd seen on Facebook, which, for the record, is not my preferred method of communication. More like Fakebook. But when the women in my life join forces it's never going to be pretty. For me, at least. And like most other times I found it easier to cave. Which left us here. Non-dancing at a barn dance. In a barn big enough for half of Trinity Lakes to brave the cold and do-si-do or whatever the heck it was they were doing.

"So, are you going to stand here all night, looking like an undertaker, or are you actually going to crack a smile?"

I look down at my black t-shirt and jeans, then let my gaze drift up her Goth-flavored attire: a black velvet top, and a black lace skirt over tights that were—you guessed it—black. Honestly, it looked like we were either well-dressed Ninjas or readying for Halloween, not New Year's Eve. "I haven't seen you getting your party on."

I think I hear her mutter the word Boomer, and I'm not exactly sure I want to know why. "Look, I came," I remind her.

"I don't think this is what Gran meant though."

"Meant about what?" I ask, suspicious.

"About finding a girlfriend."

I hope to heaven nobody has heard her. I mean, it'd be hard to, given it's louder than a roaring jet engine in here, but still. "You don't honestly expect me to find her here?"

"Why not?" An unholy grin lights her face. "Oh ye of little faith."

For a second, I wonder how a person gnashes their teeth, then I decide it's easier to just speak. "Don't you have somewhere else to be?"

She chuckles again, and even though I know it's at my expense, I'm so glad to hear it. Her laughter warms my chest like an electric blanket. "Just remember, I dare you to have fun."

I make a face at her, and she grins and ambles slowly past the red-and-white draped table, grabbing a glass filled with a drink I hope isn't inappropriate for someone underage, before resuming her seat near the band. We might both be shy, but there's something kind of bold in how Georgia owns her awkwardness, whereas I feel like awkwardness has always owned me.

A commotion at the door draws every head, and in walk three women. Young women, tanned, pretty, the youngest honey-blonde tossing her hair around like she's a celebrity, her big blue eyes zoning in on Jackson before settling on me. My skin prickles, and it's like a premonition. I've seen that kind of interest before, and I've got no interest in anyone like a Cassie again. But she's zeroing in, and as she moves closer, I can hear her voice, and it's high-pitched and holds a whine.

"Oh my gosh, it's all so cute!" She stops in front of me and, I swear, she licks her lips. "And you're so cute! G'day, I'm Lydia Bennett."

I blink. Okay, there's confident, and then there's this over-perky Australian person. "Hello."

I don't smile, and I'm vaguely aware my voice sounds like what I remember my grandfather's as being like, as stiff and formal as his house I once visited in England. Her smile dips fifty percent, and I feel like a heel, but I don't exactly want to encourage her, so I look away. Not my finest hour, I know.

Jackson is back and now doing introductions, and I freeze as Ms. Perky's older sisters draw closer. I figure they have to be sisters, as they all share similar facial features and hair color, something that's confirmed as Jackson introduces them as Jane and Elissa Bennett. The one called Jane says hello in a softer voice than her younger sister, her expression seeming a little shy. But it's the other one who eyes me in a way that makes me tense, but in a completely different way to Lydia.

"Mr. Darcy," Elissa says.

I nod but say nothing. I can't say anything, because it's like my tongue has swollen to six times its usual size. Ever since Cassie, I seem to have lost the ability to relax around pretty women. And this woman, with her deep blue eyes, and cheek-bones, and curves, and voice—that sounds far more like Cate Blanchett than Rebel Wilson—is in a class higher than Cassie, that's for sure.

"Come on, Liam," Jackson says. "Don't just stand there. Ask one of them to dance."

It's like the snow outside has entered my brain. My thoughts are trickling slower than the frozen stream that separates the Reilly ranch from my own. I can't speak, let alone ask one of them to dance. Especially as I can't dance anyway. Not that Jackson would know that. Nobody here knows that for all my so-called accomplishments, dancing was never high on my personal agenda of life goals.

So I do the only thing I can think of. Turn and walk away.

RIGHT ON CUE. Rich, full of himself and rude. So rude. Actually, I'm surprised as I thought that all Americans could at least fake politeness. But there was none of that with Liam Darcy as he walked through the crowd without uttering so much as an 'excuse me'.

"Don't mind Liam," Jackson said. "He's a bit funny like that. Right, Matt?"

Matt apparently doesn't have an opinion. He's too busy studying Jane as if she's made of gold. And Jane. Jane, the quiet, reserved, tactful and kind one of us. She's taken Matt by the hand —by the hand! —and they're off to join the dancing. Lydia is nowhere to be seen. She's not short of confidence but highly deficient in tact. I knew it was a mistake to come. I've lost control of the whole situation and we haven't been here five minutes. The worst of it, Mum and Dad have arrived with James and Marianne Kennedy. This is a family event, and while the whole purpose of me meeting my family here at Trinity Lakes during semester break was so we could spend time together, I hardly imagined that meant we'd end up at a dance. Mum is scanning the room looking very pleased with herself. Dad has retreated to the food section with James, probably to meet the locals. No doubt there are farmers here, and that will be right up Dad's alley.

"You're looking a little lost." Lucy Kennedy is standing next to me. Thank goodness she hasn't left me totally alone.

"I can't believe that Liam Darcy fellow. How rude."

Lucy smiles. "Come on, let's get something to drink, and then we can make a plan of attack."

"What are you planning to attack?"

Lucy waves her hand around the room. "The social intricacies of a country dance. We need to have a plan."

I have a plan. But I can't leave on my own. I have to rally the family so we can leave together and go back to Lakeview Lodge as a group. Fat chance of that happening now. The whole family, including Dad, are now firmly ensconced in the social intricacies.

"Come on." Lucy tugs me by the arm. "It can't be that bad."

I follow her through the crowd of strangers—well, not entirely strangers. I know all the Kennedys and there are six of them, plus Sasha's fiancé and Caleb's girlfriend. Then there are my two sisters. Jane's face is more alive with joy than I've seen in, well, forever. This is not good.

"Who's that man Lydia is dancing with? He looks too old for her."

"Mmm." Lucy frowns and I feel a sense of foreboding. "Gary Wickley. He used to work for Liam Darcy, but he left suddenly, and there are rumors they had a falling out."

"I like him already. I'm glad someone can stand up to Mr. Darcy and all his ridiculous money."

Lucy hasn't heard me, or she's pretending she hasn't heard me. My comment might have sounded a bit harsh, but really. I don't like being rejected at the best of times, but to be rejected without even a pinch of remorse, and in front of a group of people, feels a bit much.

"Here." Lucy has a cup of punch and shoves it in my hands. Perhaps that's what I need. Sugar. "Let's go and sit down over there."

I follow Lucy's pointing finger to a bunch of hay bales surrounded by tall potted plants, all decorated in twinkling lights. Out of the way of other people, it looks exactly like the spot I want to sit and examine my injured pride.

"Liam Darcy isn't all bad." Lucy is determined to get to the core of it. "Perhaps he had a sudden call of nature."

I smile. It's doubtful, but Lucy wants to give him the benefit of the doubt.

"Shhh." Lucy holds her finger to her lips. "He and Jackson are heading this way."

I can see them coming to stand on the other side of the potted plants. Looks like Jackson is going to give him a good sound talking to. Besides the fact I don't want to continue talking about him while he's in hearing distance, I also want to eavesdrop and hear what Jackson has to say. Yes, I'm mature that way.

"Honestly, Liam. You've got to work on your social grace."

"Sorry, this whole scene is overwhelming. It's really not my thing."

"You make it sound like you're a recluse. Get a grip." Jackson shoves his hands in his back pockets. "I've seen you talk all day long at one of your business forums."

"Yes, well…" Liam clears his throat.

Yes, well what, mister? I have an urge to say. Not that I will. Unlike some people, I know how to fake politeness.

"You were quite rude to the Bennett sisters when I introduced you," Jackson continues.

I exchange smirks with Lucy. You tell him, Jackson.

"They seem to have recovered," Mr. Grumpy says.

What?

"You should try to get to know them. They seem really nice."

Thank you, Jackson.

"Apart from the fact they're from Australia—"

Excuse me?

"—the eldest one seems to be quite taken with Matt Kennedy," Mr. Darcy continues, "and the younger one is way too flirtatious for my taste."

"Wow." There's a pause, as if Jackson is as gob-smacked as I am by the judgements and struggling to find something non-nuclear to say. "What about Elissa? She's the best looking of the three."

The offense heating my chest eases. I knew I liked this man.

"Looks aren't everything."

My ears burn. Did I just hear him correctly?

"Which is exactly why you should take the opportunity to get to know her a bit. That's what an event like this is for, you know." Jackson is really on his high horse now.

"She's not that good looking. She's okay, but not pretty enough to tempt me."

Wow. And that heat is climbing again, threatening to spill out my mouth. I zip my lips, clench my hands, and silently fume.

"You're a snob, Liam," Jackson finally says. "She seems nice."

"How do you know? Have you spent any time with her?"

"Not yet, but since you're going to hide in the corner, I think I'll take the opportunity."

Good luck with that, I think, unable to look at Lucy. I don't dare trust myself to talk to anyone at all.

CHAPTER 3

*S*o my plan for swapping out Mr. Serious Darcy for a Mr. Fun persona has flopped. I'm pretty sure Elissa Bennett thinks I'm the Antichrist. Which maybe I was channeling a little. Sometimes it's just too easy for filter-less me to overshare. I've always put it down to awkwardness, but I can see how some might think I'm just plain rude. Which isn't me. Not really. *Way to go, Darcy.* I grind my teeth.

At least I can be thankful nobody but Jackson heard me spouting off my stupid lies. Because they are lies. Elissa Bennett is exactly my ideal version of pretty, and exactly enough to tempt me. But I don't like feeling tempted. It makes me feel unsure, out of control, like something crazy stupid could happen. Which it just might if ever I looked too long into those eyes—eyes which hold the mystery of an evening star-lit sky.

I rub a hand over my face. I must be coming down with something. Poetry isn't me.

I hear a rustle from behind the fake ficus screening the corner. Uh oh. And when I see who it is my heart drops. Awesome. Is it possible tonight could get any worse?

I cough and try to come up with something that doesn't

sound pathetic, but I don't think anything I can ever say will un-patheticize my previous words. Elissa's chin is tilted, her top lip looks like it's curled, and those eyes I thought so lustrous and beautiful spark with obvious scorn. She walks past, as if deter-mined to leave, Lucy Kennedy trailing like a lesser star behind the sun.

"Miss Bennett."

She stops. Motionless. Still isn't looking at me.

"I, uh," really should've thought this through. "Um—" Heat is rising up my neck. Suave James Bond I am not. "I meant to say—"

"Sorry?"

Yeah, exactly that. "I really am. Sorry, I mean. I, uh—"

"I beg your pardon?" she continues, and I realize she's not prompting me to do something my mother taught me years ago.

I swallow, straighten, and will her to believe me. "Please forgive me, Miss Bennett. I expressed some things very poorly—"

"Poorly, or appallingly?" she interrupts.

Seems I'm not the only one missing some manners in this conversation. Probably won't help to point that out. "Forgive me. I didn't know you were there."

"Oh. I see." Her gaze finally swivels to meet mine, and I'm sucked into the endless blue. Endless blue holding a storm and lightning, judging from the sparks. Or is that a watery sheen? "So it's okay to say that kind of thing if people can't hear you?"

"No. Yes." I don't know anymore. What is it about this girl from Down Under that's turned my brain upside down?

Her head tilts to one side like I'm an alien muttering in a language from far, far away. And I realize I don't want those blue eyes engaged in a personal death-stare on me anymore.

"Please." I want to point out that I don't beg. Ever. Well, except to Gran and Georgia, occasionally. "Forgive me."

I see the battle on her face as her features pinch, and she

sucks in her bottom lip and chews it. I suddenly want to know just how soft that lip might be. Also not something to share right now. What can I say to prove I'm not the uncouth idiot she clearly thinks I am? "W-want to dance?" I stammer.

She blinks. Takes a step back as if she's afraid she'll be infected. "No, thank you."

Oh. The relief at her rejection—had that seriously come out of my mouth?—is followed by a ripple of regret. For while threading my eyelids with barbed wire is preferable to dancing, I can't help wishing she didn't wish me dead. Which she clearly does right now.

"Oh, go on, Elissa," Lucy nudges her. "You're going to have to forgive him."

Am I? the raised eyebrows levelled my direction imply.

Man. The woman seems to like being offended. Well, good luck to her. I shrug. Take my own step back. And nearly trip over Georgia, who murmurs a loud ouch and winces, bending to rub her just-squashed toe. "You okay?"

"Do I look okay?" Georgia grumbles, eyeing the other two women before her gaze returns to me. Her own eyebrows lift, and I subtly shake my head. Nope. Nothing to see here.

Fortunately, Elissa and Lucy seem to take this as their chance to escape, leaving me with a mix of relief and regret that I hadn't exactly put my best foot forward. Or any foot forward. Except into my mouth.

"Did I hear you ask her to dance?" Georgia murmurs.

"I don't dance."

"I know. Which is why I was so stunned when I thought I heard you say that." Her eyes widen. "You like her."

"No, I don't," I say firmly.

"Yes, you do. Why else would you ask her to dance?"

Why indeed. "She doesn't want to, so it doesn't matter."

"Wow." I see the questions whirling around her brain, as if she can't quite believe that someone would turn down her bachelor-of-the-year brother. She shoots another look at Elissa, now standing on the sidelines next to Lucy, both watching as the dancing crowd's foot stomps and yee-ha's increase in volume.

"I dare you," Georgia says.

My attention returns to my sister's face. "What?"

She has a wicked grin. "I dare you to ask her to dance again."

"Are you out of your mind? She's already said no."

"I dare you," she repeats.

I shake my head, wondering if we can leave before midnight. Surely the fact I showed up at all should score some brownie points, right?

"Liam." Jackson's smile softens as he sees GG. "Hey, Georgia. It's good to see you here."

"Hi." She offers a small smile. He's about the only guy she tolerates, but even with him it's only for a short time. One day she'll put the past behind her.

"What are we going to do about getting your brother to dance?" Jackson nudges me.

"He's about to ask that girl"—she points to Elissa—"to dance."

"Is he now?" Jackson chuckles. "I never thought I'd see the day."

"Liam?" my sister says. Commands, really. How is she so good at that?

"Fine." A dare is a dare, even if it is my kryptonite.

I steel my spine—come on, I've faced down Russian oligarchs, I can take on an Aussie girl—and move beside Elissa again.

But before I can speak, Jackson's doing the talking for me. "Elissa, I'd really feel like I'm a bad host if I didn't see you dancing."

"Oh, I'm perfectly fine watching," she protests.

Just then the music quietens, and the dance caller grabs the microphone. "Okay everyone. It's time for one of the highlights of the night. The Flying Dutchman!"

"The Flying what?" Elissa asks.

"Grab the two people nearest you, and get out onto the dance floor," the caller continues. "One guy with two girls, or two guys and one girl, it's up to you."

I'm tempted to scuttle away like Lucy had the brains to do, but Jackson stops me, gently pushing me closer to Elissa.

"There you go," Jackson says with a sly grin. "I guess that's your cue."

The expression on Elissa's face hovers between dismay and outrage, and I know my face is probably little better.

"I thought there had to be three people," she says, her glance around holding more than a trace of desperation. "Where's Lucy?"

"Look who I found." It's Jackson again, encouraging a reluctant-looking Lucy to my side. "Now Liam, remember how this is done?"

I shoot him my best are-you-stupid look. Of course I don't remember. I look longingly at the door.

"What is the Flying Dutchman?" Elissa mutters.

"Just follow along," Jackson says soothingly. "It's easy."

I grit my teeth and somehow find myself trapped between the two women, neither of whom seem eager to follow the caller's instructions to wrap their arms around my waist. The caller explains this is a traditional dance done around these parts, and I'm wondering just how traditional something can be if I've never heard of it, when the music starts.

Apparently we have to move forward slowly around a large circle, our line of three moving in unison, which is hard when one woman is significantly shorter than my six foot two, and the other would obviously prefer to only touch me via a ten foot pole. But I'm not so averse to holding her, my senses tracking Elissa's scent—something waterlily-like and cool—and I have to force myself not to tighten my hold. Somehow we manage to do the kick mostly in time, and I'm relieved that Elissa doesn't feel the need to kick me. The music's got a slow kind of polka feel, and I'm almost thinking I've got the hang of this dancing thing —look out John Travolta—when suddenly the music and dancing speeds up into carnival land. Around us, triplets break up into pairs, the middle guy or girl locking arms and swinging around first one of their partners, then the other.

Naturally, I turn to Lucy, as Elissa's gaze still holds daggers, and I manage to swing her around like the others are doing before returning to the center. I glance at Elissa, and crook my arm and I hear the sigh that seems to have come from the bottom of her feet.

She links arms and we carefully spin. Carefully, because she seems to be doing her best to not touch me any more than is absolutely necessary.

We return to our original positions and follow the pattern again. Slow progression, kick, slow progression, then fast do-si-do.

We do this another two times, and each time the band plays the fast part just a little faster. I glance across and see Georgia has got her phone out and is filming me, and I grimace at her. She just laughs and keeps recording.

Elissa is moving stiffly, and I'm wondering just how much longer we have to do this when the music picks up speed again. But this time feels a bit too fast, and I'm unsteady on my feet as I return from whirling Lucy around. Now it's Elissa's turn, and as I hold out my arm she's frowning up at me. My chest knots, and she places her arm within the loop of mine, and we start to swing around. But we're going too fast, whirling around and around and around, and somehow my feet stumble. I try to regain my steps, but my grip fails, and before I know what's happening, Elissa is flying off to crash into a nearby group, and the three of them crash to the floor.

There's a scream, a yell, and the music halts. Lucy gasps and runs to Elissa's aid.

Leaving me standing there, alone, the heat of extreme mortification burning my cheeks as every eye turns my way. Who knew the Flying Dutchman would actually lead to a flying Australian?

"Liam!" Georgia's agonized whisper snaps me back to awareness, and I hurry to offer a hand to Elissa.

"I'm so sorry," I murmur.

But she avoids my eyes and ignores my hand, accepting Jackson's assistance to rise instead. And I know I'm never going to live this night down.

Happy New Year?

Oh boy. Hardly.

"Jane." I snap my fingers in front of her sleepy face. She rolls over, her cheek smooshed on the pink ruffled pillowcase. "Hello. Are you with me?"

"What?"

Jane's sweet smile is so disarming. How can I be annoyed with her? It's not really her fault anyway. I sigh.

"Elissa?" Now she's trying to get me to focus, since I've drifted into a rewind of last night.

"That was the worst night of my life." I can still see the blurred faces of the other dancers as I flew through the air—faces that soon became very clear, decorated with looks of concern. My pride was not just injured, it was flattened by a steamroller, and it was doubtful it would ever regain its former shape.

"It wasn't that bad, Elissa. Nobody thought anything of it." Jane's tone is always so infuriatingly calm, and her logic is usually quite accurate, but not this time.

"I was the center of attention, in a pile of unladylike arms and legs."

"You were wearing jeans. It's not like you had a skirt flung up over your head."

"Jaaaane." I lie back on the pillow and put my head on her shoulder. I'm in desperate need of somebody to empathize with me.

"You must have been embarrassed, and I'm sorry—" Jane gives me a squeezy hug—"but you have to look at the bright side."

I pull back and straighten. There was a bright side? That seemed unlikely, but Jane is well known for her optimism. I'm waiting for her to enlighten me. It had better be good, because all I really want is the sympathetic hugs and promise of comfort chocolate. My eyebrows are about to disappear off the top of my head—she's taking a long time to get to the point—then I notice her eyebrows are also raised in that you-know-what-I'm-talking-about look.

"What bright side?" I'm about to skip it and go straight for the fridge.

"You were dancing with Liam Darcy."

Was there something here I'd missed?

"Don't look at me with that frown on your face." Jane is in lecture mode. Only she can deliver a blow covered in sugar and angel-dust. "Every woman in the room was hoping to dance with Liam Darcy, yet you were the only person he asked."

I wanted to ask how she knew the minds of fifty-odd women, but that was not as important as changing the course of where this was going.

"I was the only woman he asked, and then he literally dumped me in the middle of the dance floor."

"I'm sure it was an accident."

"I told you what he said about me when he didn't know I was listening."

Jane's forehead had developed the tiniest frown—indiscernible and unremarkable on anyone else, but on Jane, it was the harshest of criticisms.

"Elissa Bennett. You were eavesdropping, and you know what they say about eavesdroppers."

I don't actually, but don't bother to tell her. I'm sure it's some tidy little proverb that condemns those who listen at keyholes. But I wasn't really listening at a keyhole. I was sitting in a lovely little nook enjoying a rest, minding my own business. How could I help it if he lumbered across and started shouting insults in my direction?

"He singled you out, and you should take that as a huge compliment. Matt said he rarely goes to social events, and he doesn't recall having ever seen him dance before."

I shouldn't wonder. If last night's attempt was anything to go by, I'd say it's best if he stays well away from any unsuspecting young women.

The door flies open, and Lydia wanders in, rubbing her eyes and yawning.

"You two are up early." She flops onto Jane's bed, picks up a pink fluffy pillow and hugs it to herself.

"It's nearly midday." Jane's tone is its usual kindness in decibels. "What time did you get home?"

"Gary Wickley gave me a ride home around four a.m."

"What?" I'm up straight and alert. "Does Dad know?"

"Stop fussing, Elissa. Mum said it was fine as long as we were in a group."

"Lydia."

I turn and stare at Jane. Her tone has developed something I've never heard before. I can't identify it, but it sounds ominous.

"Gary Wickley is too old for you. You should be careful." Is this the Jane I know?

"How do you know?" Lydia has defensiveness sparking in her eyes.

"Matt told me. He's nearly twenty-nine."

"So? I'm nearly nineteen. That's only ten years' difference. Dad is twelve years older than Mum."

"Yes." I want to say, *let that be a lesson to you,* but I'm not sure Lydia would understand.

"It's not a crime. What's your problem?" Lydia might legally be considered an adult in Australia, but she has the emotional maturity of a ten-year-old. Still, I don't want to be mean to her.

"Matt said Gary was dismissed from his job at Darcy's ranch." Jane is quoting Matt Kennedy like he is Obi-Wan Kenobi.

"And that's another thing," Lydia shoots accusations in my direction.

My shoulders straighten up another couple of centimeters, bracing for a barrage.

"Gary told me about being fired. It was … a different name to what we use in Australia, but the same as unfair dismissal, and Liam Darcy owes him thousands of dollars and refuses to pay."

Her glare is full of fire. "And how is this my fault?"

"*You* had the audacity to dance with him." Lydia gets up from Jane's bed and throws the fluffy pink pillow down in a whoosh. "I don't think you have any right to be making judgements when the man you chose is far worse!"

As Lydia flounces out of the room, I pick my jaw up from the floor. In my defense, it was Jane who was throwing out the cautions—most un-Jane like—and secondly, I'd hardly call that disastrous dance anything resembling me making a connection with Liam Darcy. In fact, hearing Gary Wickley's account of unfair dismissal only adds to my dislike of his former boss.

"I'm sorry, Elissa." Jane is incredible. She's so sensitive, and her uncharacteristic moment of stern admonition is quickly hidden by her remorse.

"It's not your fault. Gary Wickley *is* too old for Lydia. Mum shouldn't have allowed her to stay on her own."

"But he's not too old for you."

I smile. I love Jane's eternal optimism—always looking for the silver lining.

"It is true, there's only a three year difference, but I might add, we are here in Trinity Lakes for a family holiday. I have zero intention of trying to find a man, despite yours and Mum's best efforts. Let's just enjoy the Bennett family reunion while we have the opportunity."

We spend a few minutes getting dressed and I help Jane with the curling iron, giving her lovely hair some bounce and body.

"Are you planning on seeing Matt Kennedy again?" I give her a wink. Instead of protesting, that soft pink climbs in her cheeks again. "Are you serious about him, Jane?"

"I remember him from school when they used to live in Australia. He's really nice, Elissa. I had a really good time with him last night."

Apart from the fact I want to point out her overuse of the word 'really,' I can't help but feel pleased. The Kennedys are a nice family whom we have known for years. But despite his five years in Australia, he is American.

I couldn't bear the thought of Jane marrying and staying here in the States when I intend to go back to Australia after I've finished my time at Seattle University.

But I'm not going to borrow trouble. The Jane-Matt thing might be a holiday romance that fizzles as quickly as it started.

By the time we get to the kitchen, Mum and Dad are sitting down enjoying a cup of tea.

"Lydia has suggested we meet at the Bellbird Café in town for lunch," Mum says; her enthusiasm in direct contrast to Dad's look of resigned frustration. "I think it's a wonderful idea."

I can't see why Dad is so opposed. Perhaps he's not opposed and I've misread his expression.

"Great. Let's go. I don't want to be late." Lydia bounces out of the room.

Late? Late for what?

Mum and Lydia seem to have a spiritual connection. Whenever Lydia gets an idea in her head, Mum becomes her champion and personal assistant in getting the rest of us on board. So under Mum's nagging tone, we bundle into the rental car and punch the directions into the GPS. Why? I have no idea. Trinity Lakes is hardly a bustling metropolis. Apart from the pretty lakes there is a Hallmark-worthy main street lined with Christmas-decorated stores and quaint streetlamps and hanging baskets with trailing ivy. A number of streets fan out from this, aptly named First, Second, Third, Fourth, Fifth and Sixth Street. The Bellbird Café is on Main Street, and it takes us exactly forty-five seconds to get there, and three seconds to find a parking space. If we were in Australia, we would have walked. But it is snowing, and as a family of Australians from a semi-arid region of the country, snow is a wondrous and unknown variable, and far better approached from the comfort of a warm vehicle.

Lydia is obviously hungry as she's almost strangled herself trying to leap out before she's undone her seatbelt.

"Crazy girl."

Did Dad just mumble something? Huh. I'm guessing he would preferred to have stayed in front of the fire at the Lakeview Lodge and read. Still, we have to eat.

By the time we get inside, I'm knocked over by the charm of the atmosphere. Mismatched tables and chairs, wooden floors, tealight candles aglow in a variety of glassware. Hand painted china plates on the butter yellow walls, the shelves lined with vintage teacups and teapots galore, like a dozen Nannas had got together and flung their collectables on the walls. Then I hear it.

Something that sounds like rainforest music that holds that tinkle of an Australian bellbird. The sound is so unexpected, I feel my soul ease. What an enchanting place, like a pocket of home in the midst of Americana. A wave of homesick nostalgia creases my chest as I smile. What a lovely idea of Lydia's to come here.

I look around for Lydia who seems to have disappeared down the back of the restaurant. Then I see that this is not just a lovely idea. Lydia has pre-arranged a meeting with Gary Wickley.

"Be kind," Jane whispers in my ear.

"I will be perfectly kind." For starters, I want to find out about this dismissal saga.

I'm just about to go to the table that seems to have been reserved for us when the bell over the door rings. I turn to see who else has happened out on New Year's Day for a bite of lunch, and my stomach tenses while my thoughts whiz around in a flashback of last evening's embarrassing Flying Dutchman. Liam Darcy has walked in. Wonderful. He gives a weak smile in my direction.

Really? A smile? I'm not impressed.

CHAPTER 4

*M*y attempt at conciliation drains away at the return of Ms. Dagger Eyes. Although, to be fair, I can't really blame her. I was certainly not my best-self last night. In any way. So I can't blame her for disliking me.

I turn to my sister and grandmother who have both escaped the cold from outside and are standing in the entry, shrugging off their heavy coats, and wonder if it's too late to suggest we go somewhere else. Not that I'm afraid of a certain forthright Aussie with golden brown hair. It'd just be nice, before I head off for business meetings tomorrow, to not have reminders of last night's failures ruin today.

My sister's hitch of breath draws my attention, and I follow her slack-jawed expression to see another person seated at the Bennett's table. Another person, who looks an awful lot like someone who provokes strong negative emotions.

I move in front facing Georgia, to screen her view of him. "We don't have to eat here," I murmur.

"But my dear boy, I want to eat here," Gran complains. "Brenda has the day off, and I've heard the poached eggs are the best in town. And I think the décor quite delightful."

My sister and I have a wordless conversation, mostly involving eyes and hitched brows. We've never told Gran the full story of why Wickley got fired. If we had, I suspect the man would've been drawn and quartered by sundown. But the fact he's still hanging around town means Georgia is going to have to face him sooner or later. I'd rather it be here when I can back her up, rather than one of the many times when I'm not, and she's taken by surprise. Who knows how many more months of therapy she'd need to have?

"Up to you, Georgia," I murmur. "Your choice."

I say that last word deliberately, a reminder of what the counselor had said. Georgia has the power to choose—the choice to forgive and own her right to live freely in this town, or the choice to let the man continue to dominate her emotions and movement. I'm praying she chooses option A.

Her scared eyes meet mine, and she offers the slightest nod. Bars in my chest ease, and I clench a fist in victory, before wrapping her in the quickest of hugs. "You've got this," I remind her.

"You sure?" Doubt loads her words, her expression.

"Can we please eat?" Gran moves to a nearby table and drags out a chair, before plonking down her purse on another wooden seat. "I'm hungry."

Georgia clears her throat, like she's clearing away a load of emotion, and I don't miss the fact she chooses to sit facing away from the Bennetts. And their companion.

Which leaves me the only spare seat so I'm facing them. Which isn't my preference either. But it's not all because of concerns about my sister and he-who-shan't-be-named. It's also about just why Elissa and her family are spending time with someone who, if I hadn't had it drilled into me that family pride matters most, I should've reported to the police long ago. I scowl at him, hating how he's hurt my sister, hating the fact he's gotten away with things. I did what I could, but my sister's insistence on wanting to keep things hush hush meant my hands were tied. But I hadn't let that stop me from using certain college boxing skills Gran never knew about and employing a few ranch hands as undercover guards. There is no way that man is ever coming onto our property again.

I grind my teeth and force myself to look at the laminated menu, conscious there's a waitress waiting to take my order.

"I'll have the blueberry and yoghurt granola, thanks." Yeah, I know it's lunch, not breakfast, but after last night's late hour, this is my first meal of the day. And it looks like I'll need something more fortifying than a fluffy flapjack guaranteed to cause a mid-afternoon sugar crash.

"Something to drink?"

I order a cappuccino—the coffee here is as good as anything I've had in Italy—and settle back in my chair. I try to pay attention to whatever GG and Gran are talking about, but my eyes keep straying to the laughing family over there. How can they not know how bad that man is? I'm half tempted to jump up and tell them but figure any explanations would embarrass GG more than it's worth. So instead I silently fume, clenching and unclenching my hands, my knee jerking up and down under the table. It's probably a good thing I'm going on a work trip to New York tomorrow, because the agitation inside is making me want to punch something—someone—again.

"You okay, Liam?" Georgia asks, her forehead pleated.

I jerk a nod and manage a tight smile.

"You don't need to worry. I'm okay," she says.

I nod, and hope my smile conveys reassurance. But I feel full of regret, full of what-if's, wishing I was somehow smarter and had managed to convince Georgia to report him. But time had kept dragging on, and now I wondered if she was reaching that point where to be dragged through it all would do more harm than good.

A loud hiss of the espresso machine cuts through the clamor, forcing conversations to quieten. I sneak a peek at the Bennett table, frowning as I see Wickley look away. Then notice Elissa Bennett glance at me, then back at him, then back at me.

Her blue gaze holds shards of ice, and fresh regrets consume me, as I wonder what I can ever do to make up for last night's travesty. Flowers? A dinner? An island getaway—without my unwelcome presence?

Why that last thought knots my chest I don't want to investigate, and I'm relieved as the coffee machine buzz falls quiet and conversation can distract me again. Until I hear Wickley's low rumbly voice followed by the brazen youngest Bennett's screech of laughter.

"Some people should be more considerate of others." If Gran believed in rolling her eyes she probably would be, judging from that tone of voice.

Call me judgy, but I kind of get the impression that Lydia Bennett has never really considered another person in her life. She seems made from the same self-centered mold as Cassandra Bellingham. Vain. Money hungry. Chasing men.

"Some people probably haven't benefited from time in America's top boarding school for girls," I suggest, appealing to my grandmother's well-honed sense of family pride.

"Indeed."

I swap glances with Georgia, who does nothing to hide her eye-roll. She did not attend the same school as my grandmother, something which causes no end of lamenting from Gran.

Fortunately, distraction is provided by an elderly woman with suspiciously brown hair who insists on talking to Gran. Which leaves GG and me to shrug and both pull out our phones. I've determined to do better this year, and after a no-phone—well, barely any phone—Christmas and New Year's Eve, I'm kind of enjoying not feeling like I need to be chained to the thing. A quick scan of my email reveals nothing urgent, although I make a mental note to get on to the Burundi project manager and see if we can get that started sooner. By yesterday would've been nice.

I stuff my phone back in my pocket. I don't want to be tempted to keep scrolling and be sucked into the time warp that business often leads to, where I answer one email and look up to discover hours have gone by. GG is right. I do need more fun in my life.

A glance around the space and it's hard not to notice the Bennetts sitting two tables away, smiling, looking like they were born to have fun. Even if one was over-screechy, and the mother was almost as bad, and one of them seemed to hold a penchant for scowls I really wish I didn't deserve.

"Oh my gosh."

Georgia's murmur thankfully draws my attention. She's looking at her phone, something non-Gran approved, but Gran is still talking to another customer.

"What's up?" I ask.

"You won't like it," she cautions.

I gesture for the phone anyway.

She bites her lip and slowly slides her phone to me where a video from last night taunts. I press play, thankful it's on silent, because these pictures are telling way more than a thousand words. Air leaves my lungs, and nausea fills my gut.

"It wasn't me, I promise," GG says.

"I know," I reassure.

But God help the person who did. Someone must hate me a lot. I glance up at the Bennett table, scowling at the man who I know does hate me, and my gaze accidentally collides with my unlucky dance partner. Elissa instantly looks away, but I know those icicles mentally being flung my way are thoroughly deserved.

I only hope she never knows that someone posted the flying Australian on YouTube.

~

"You're joking." I don't know why Gary Wickley would try to jest, but what else could I say to his long and pathetic tale of woe?

"I'm completely serious." Gary has all of us hanging on his every word. "Liam Darcy thinks he is above the law and can treat people however he wishes, just because he has the money and power to do so."

"He's watching us." Lydia gives a silly nervous giggle. "I hope he doesn't come over here and start a fight."

"Surely not."

Mum is so gullible. Even I doubt that Liam Darcy is the sort of person to put on a public display that would have the whole room watching. On the other hand, the memory of last night's inelegant fiasco ending with me bowling another set of dancers over like ten pins has me entertaining the idea of fisticuffs between Darcy and Wickley. I smile at the prospect of Darcy eating dirt.

"Don't be silly, Lydia." Dad's caution is in his usual mellow tone, and it is doubtful that either Lydia or Mum have heard him.

"I think there must have been a misunderstanding." Jane can't help but play the diplomat. It's ingrained in her nature. "Matt speaks very highly of Liam Darcy."

"Yes, well, he would." Gary's tone retains the contempt he's had all along. "Matt and his brother Caleb are friends with the Darcys."

"You say that like it is a fault in the Kennedys." I can't help challenging Gary. He seems very quick to feed off the misery he allegedly lives at the hands of the supposed tyrant.

"No, the Kennedys are good people, and they don't really know Darcy like I do."

"How well do you know him?" I ask.

"I've worked at their ranch since junior high, after school for an allowance."

"Well, there, you see. That sounds like he has a kind heart." Jane sits back, with a smile, obviously relieved.

"No, that was his grandfather who hired me. Darcy senior was a truly great man. His grandson, however…"

"Who is the girl with him?" I'm curious. Liam is attentive to the pretty young woman who's sitting with her back to us. I'd noticed her last night as well.

"That's his sister, Georgia. She and I used to be good friends until Darcy stepped in and broke up our friendship."

"Why would he do that?" Lydia is buying Gary's sorry story. I'm still reserving my opinion.

"He's a control freak. Georgia is a great kid, but he won't let her out of the house alone. She doesn't have a life of her own."

"That's awful," Lydia said.

"Surely, you must have misunderstood things." Jane again. She can't bear to have anyone be a bad guy.

"I wish I had misunderstood. But I know only too well. He's controlling and dishonest."

"How so, young man? How is Liam Darcy dishonest?" Dad has finally found enough volume in his voice to be heard.

"He'd rather buy a private jet than pay what he owes me, and I'm not so flush with cash that I can afford to let it go."

"A private jet?" Now my hackles are raised. I've spent years studying and working in the area of environment and sustainability, and a private jet is the very opposite of minding one's carbon footprint.

"He flies all over the place for who knows what reason."

"Business?" Dad is not sold on Gary's story.

"So he says. But if he was doing so well in business, he could afford to pay me what's owed."

I can't help but glance in the direction of the Darcys. Liam keeps staring in my direction. What is that look in his eye?

Whatever it is, I'm not impressed. Fancy owning a private jet. He probably also has a million cows who rip up the land and release methane gas into the atmosphere. Money doesn't impress me, buddy. No, sir, it does not.

The discussion at our table is disturbed by a server coming up with the check.

"I'll get this." Gary is certainly a generous sort of person. He's doing his best to charm Dad, with limited success. I know Dad. He's not easily charmed. Mum and Lydia, on the other hand, are Gary's devoted groupies as evidenced by their dreamy, drooling expressions.

The server is only away a couple of minutes and she's back. She is trying to speak quietly to Gary, but we can all hear. "I'm sorry, sir, but this card has been declined."

"What?" Gary is all offended. "Try it again."

"I'm sorry, sir. I tried it three times."

"This is ridiculous. You see?" He glares in Liam's direction. "If that man would pay me what he owes, this sort of thing wouldn't happen."

Dad surreptitiously gives his credit card to the girl.

"Don't forget to include a tip," Gary says.

"What?" Mum sits up straight and looks alarmed.

"A tip. Twenty percent should cover it." Gary waves the girl away.

"A tip! What on earth do you mean by that?"

"Mum," I caution quietly. She's only been in the country a few days and not used to the custom. Most Australians are outraged when they're not expecting it.

"Why should we pay twenty percent more? The prices are on the menu. I'll pay what I owe!"

"Mum. Stop. The wait staff don't get the same sort of wages like they do in Australia."

"Well, the manager should pay them properly and leave the customers alone. If they say it's fifteen dollars on the menu, then it should be fifteen dollars. If they want it to be eighteen dollars, then put that price on the menu. It's ridiculous!"

For the first time in my life, I actually agree with my mother —and I'm impressed she can calculate twenty percent without a pencil and paper. But this is America, and as they say, when in Rome...

"You just have to get used to the system." I admit it took me a while, but I've stopped hyperventilating over the surprise of being slugged an extra hidden twenty percent. Realizing just how little American servers in the hospitality industry get paid has soothed my indignation. Maybe after seven months I'm getting used to living in America.

We get up and start wrapping up with coats and scarves.

"Will you say hello to Liam as you go past?" Lydia has little tact and I watch for Gary's reaction to the question.

"I don't have a problem with him, but if he wants to talk, he can apologize to me first."

Gary waves Lydia forward, then drops back close enough to speak directly to me. "I hope you'll be able to find some time to go out for a coffee while you're here. I'd love to get to know you more."

My ego and my good sense get up to start a fight. He's just schmoozed his way through a date with Lydia, and before she's even out the door, he's switched targets. I'm tempted to be flattered, but I can't help but take into consideration the presumption of offering to pay, and then passing it off to Dad without a second thought. I know I don't like Liam Darcy, but I'm not sure I'm willing to run into the arms of Gary Wickley either.

Probably best I concentrate on enjoying our family time before I need to return to study in Seattle.

I am standing right by the Darcy table as the rest of the family are exiting the restaurant and I can't help stealing another glance—and I'm met with the most wonderful chocolate brown eyes I've ever seen. He's offering me a tentative smile. My traitorous face smiles back.

"I hope you had a nice lunch." Liam's body language and tone seem so genuine in contrast to the last hour and a half of listening to Gary's whingeing and moaning.

I nod to Liam and walk briskly out into the freezing winter air. Aah. That icy slap in the face is just what I need. I almost had a moment of emotional connection—with an environmental vandal. Phew. That was close.

"Elissa!" I'm not sure if Lydia's call is a squeal, shriek, or her normal summons, but I look up to see her waving her phone at me. "You're all over social media."

"What?" I take her phone and look at the post where I see #ElissaBennett #LiamDarcy #FlyingAustralian. I don't have to press play on the video to know someone has uploaded filmed evidence of the most embarrassing moment of my life.

"He's probably got that from his sister." Gary is now looking over my shoulder. "That would be just like him to pull such a demeaning stunt."

Chocolate eyes be blowed. What a detestable thing to do. Even without the carbon footprint thing, Liam Darcy was now at the top of my most-never-want-to-date-ever list.

CHAPTER 5

"*T*hanks, Jarome. It looks like it's coming together really well."

"That it is, Mr. Darcy." Jarome Smith nods.

I can't help but contrast the sunny warmth of the Burundi plains showing on the screen with the heaped snow of a freak ice-storm that has stranded my plane here in the Tri-cities.

"The people are very excited," Jarome says.

I smile. Supplying water to remote villages was something I first got involved with back in my college days. Now the Pemberley Green Foundation has supplied over two hundred villages in Africa with access to clean drinking water. It still kind of shocks me that we can spend so lavishly on stuff that ultimately breaks or fades, but there are people in the world dying because they have to drink contaminated water. Jarome is the lead project officer in central Africa, and great at rallying support. It probably helps that he's not an imported white person telling the locals how to do things.

"Keep me informed," I say, before offering a farewell and ending the video call.

I send a quick email to the foundation's CEO and chief financial officer, then close my laptop, not wanting to be guilted into any other work. It's enough to sit here quietly with enough space carved out to think. To think for a moment about what I want to do with my life.

And what I think I want to do is to visit Jarome, to see the dollars the foundation has raised, in action in Africa. Yeah. The more I think about it the more excited I become. Normally I am so filled with facts and figures that I don't tend to pay attention to my gut impulses. But this feels right, feels like something I should do, something I *need* to do. Something that gets me away from here.

I glance out the window, see the snow which means we'll likely be here for another few hours yet. Normally after any time away from business I'm raring to get back into things. But this past week I've had trouble staying focused, distracted by blue eyes and regrets, and wondering how I can make things up to her. If only that stupid video hadn't been leaked.

I've got to admit, it's not pleasant finding out you're trending on social media.

Ben Morrow, my New York lawyer, seemed to take a great deal of pleasure in pointing it out to me several days ago. "Who knew the cool, calm, collected William Darcy took delight in flinging girls around?"

I was half tempted to fire him, but it would be a pain to have to re-train someone else to my expectations. Although obviously he didn't get the memo because he's definitely not meeting my expectations by making comments like that.

"It wasn't like that," I'd mumbled, and tried to steer the conversation back to the topic of the benefits of Pemberley Enterprises investing in permaculture, something Georgia had pleaded with me to investigate a year or two ago, saying if I really cared about people the way I said I did, then it was important to leave the planet in a healthier state.

I couldn't disagree and was pleasantly surprised to find several other financial and environmental benefits in supporting sustainable agricultural practices. But those benefits came at the cost of a lawyer prone to making personal remarks at inopportune times. Not that I ever do that. I grimace.

"Liam?"

My head snaps up to meet Jackson's gaze. His brow is wrinkled, like he's concerned.

"You okay?"

"Sure."

He sits opposite me, stretching out his long jeans-clad legs and cowboy boots as if preparing for the cramped conditions of the next plane. "I didn't expect to see you here."

"Plane got diverted, thanks to that." I gesture to the window where steadily banking gray clouds indicate a huge storm is approaching. I'm starting to wonder whether I'd be better off finding a hotel and trying to fly home again tomorrow.

"That sure ain't pretty." He sighs.

"How's business?" I ask.

He shrugs. "Ranching is tough, you know?" A ghost of a grin crosses his face. "Although, you probably don't. For *most* of us ranching is tough, let's say."

"How's your mom these days?"

He winces. "Not great."

"I'm sorry I missed her the other night."

"She was happy to leave it to us younger folk. Her words," he adds.

I nod. "And your brother?"

"Which one?"

That's right. Jackson has three brothers. I always forget the first-born Reilly son went east a long time ago to a gardening company in the Independence Islands off South Carolina. "Dermott?"

"Married. Got a kid on the way. They came for Christmas

for the first time in years. Good to have them there. Cooper came up from California as well."

"Nice. And what about Mitchell?"

"He's enjoying playing for Minnesota."

Mitchell plays pro hockey. "Would he ever want to play for Seattle?"

"Maybe one day. I think he's happy where he is at the moment. If he moved closer to home I think he worries there might be expectations from Mom about settling down."

Oh, how well Liam knew those feelings. "My grandmother is just the same."

"I bet." Jackson's small smile held an edge of wryness.

But no way was I telling him about my grandmother's ultimatum. She'd mentioned something about it again on New Year's Day, when she'd caught me looking at Elissa Bennett, and wondered aloud about what I could possibly find interesting about that loud-mouthed family.

How to explain I couldn't stop thinking about how I'd— literally—let her down?

The thought propelled me to thinking again about what I could do to make things up to her—to them. Perhaps Jackson might have a clue.

"So, um, about your party."

Jackson chuckled. "Dude. Did you know you have your own hashtag?"

I did? "What is it?"

"Hashtag Darcy Dump."

I winced, and Jackson's laughter grew.

"Look, I know it's not very flattering—"

Try not flattering at all.

"—but what do they say in business? Any publicity is better than none."

"I think in this case I'd rather there be none," I said dryly.

"I bet."

I cleared my throat. "So, uh, how do you know the Bennett family?"

"I don't really. It's more the Kennedys who know them. I just invited them along. Why?"

So this had the potential to get awkward. "Oh I, er, just felt like I should do something to make it up to her—them," I correct myself. "The whole Bennett family, I mean."

Jackson eyed me. "I got that the first time."

Phew. "I just feel bad about how that all went, so I wanted to make sure there were no hard feelings."

"Uh huh." Jackson slouched in his seat, still gazing at me with a disconcerting look in his eye. "So what were you thinking?"

"I don't know. A meal? An invitation to go horse riding?" I shrug, suddenly feeling like my collar is really tight. "What would you suggest?"

"Well, if I was them, tourists from another country, I'd be thinking an invitation to your ranch would be really awesome." His mouth curled up on one side. "It's not the usual spread, that's for sure."

Meaning like his. The Darcy estate was about four times the size of the Reilly's ranch, and while the depths of winter weren't exactly prime time to enjoy the sights of hills, the forest, and river bends, there was enough in the main house itself to while away a few fun hours. My grandfather had designed the house to appeal to international guests, so apart from the many bedrooms, there were lots of living spaces designed specifically for people to relax and connect. The library rivaled many I've seen in England, as did the billiards room, which had proved perfect to discuss business deals. Even the indoor pool had served its purpose in building and refreshing convivial relationships.

"Seeing as they're Aussies, they might enjoy checking out your pool in the middle of winter." Jackson added a grin. "I bet it's different for them, having a swim while looking out on snow."

My pulse thumped. But while the idea of seeing Elissa in a swimsuit held a certain appeal, this wasn't about myself so much as helping her see I'm not such a bad guy.

"Maybe a simple dinner to start off with," I suggest.

"Sounds good," Jackson said.

I grab a few pertinent numbers from him and plug them into my phone. Then Jackson's phone starts buzzing, and he mutters an apology as he takes the call.

Hmm. A dinner. Where I can apologize and hopefully make Miss Elissa Bennett see me in a better light. My heart thuds again, remembering that small, unexpected smile she'd offered as she'd exited the Bellbird Café last week, a smile that had fueled warmth and led me to wonder what a full smile from Miss Elissa Bennett would look like. Maybe there was some hope for her to see me in a better light one day, after all.

LYDIA'S WILD, ecstatic expressions of enthusiasm were grating on my nerves. Especially in response to this latest idea.

"I thought you disliked Liam Darcy," I say, holding my lips firm in an attempt to reveal nothing. One thing I was sure of, I disliked Liam Darcy, and this unexpected invitation— forwarded from the Kennedys via Messenger, no less—was most unwelcome.

"Who cares about Liam Darcy? I just want to see his fabulous house. Gary told me all about it. The Darcys have an indoor swimming pool with a hot tub and sauna."

"It's the middle of winter, Lydia."

We don't do indoor pools in our part of Australia, and I

personally never venture toward the community swimming pool unless the day is well over 35 degrees Celsius—95 in Fahrenheit. My internal Australian to American converter is operating even when I don't need it to. Whatever, it has to be so hot I can fry an egg on the pavement before I consider putting on my bathers—swimsuit. Aargh. I've been in America too long. The language thing is getting to me.

"This is very kind of him." Jane is looking at the message on her phone.

Mr. Darcy has sent a group message and though it didn't come directly from him to us, it mentioned us Bennetts particularly. It makes me wonder why he bothered to include us. Apart from one smile, it's not like the man has ever been very nice to me or my family before. Exhibit A: the bruises decorating my legs from New Year's Eve.

"And he's invited Matt as well." Jane has gone all dreamy again.

I don't have the heart to point out that since he's invited Matt, and half the Kennedys, as well as Jackson Reilly, that proves this invitation is not directed at her or for her benefit.

Something hits me in the back of the head—something awfully like a wake-up call. This invitation is not on my behalf either, and certainly not because Liam Darcy with his gorgeous chocolate-brown eyes cares about me or any of us. He's having a dinner party. Reality check: his personal assistant probably sent the message.

"I'm not sure I want to go poking around the homes of the rich and famous." I quash a stupid jolt of anticipation. Or was it curiosity? Yes, definitely curiosity. What is there to anticipate?

"Well, you can stay back if you like, but I'm going." Lydia claps her hands together and squeals. Yes, it is definitely a squeal —a very annoying, child-like display of eagerness to jump into any hare-brained scheme the minute it is proposed.

"I don't see why you should be so difficult about this." Mum has been observing the conversation. "This is a wonderful opportunity for your sisters to meet some eligible young men in a social setting. You too," she says to me, "if you'd stop being so hard to get on with."

"Have you thought that meeting eligible young men might lead to a relationship, which might lead to something permanent, and then where would you be?" I know exactly where she'd be. Stuck on the other side of the world. Which mightn't be such a bad thing, now I think on it. Hmm. But clearly my mother hasn't thought this through, which is true to form.

"Well, girls," Mum ignores my question, "I think this sounds like a lovely evening out. I'm sure it's going to be fancy. Someone so rich is sure to provide a lavish spread. It's likely to be six, possibly seven courses! And we'll be dining in a fancy dining room with linen tablecloths and silver and crystal, just like a scene from *Dynasty*. Can you imagine?"

Nope. Sounds pretentious to me. "The message said a meal, Mum, not a black tie and tuxedo reception dinner."

"There is no need for you to take that tone with me," my mother huffs. "Hmm. I wonder if he has servants?" She is deliberately talking to Jane and Lydia, her back now to me. "What have you got to wear?"

More squealing. Lord, help me, I'm going to burst an eardrum if I have to be subjected to much more of this.

"Come on, Elissa." Sensitive Jane has come around to encourage me. She knows I've an emotional conundrum brewing inside. "I know Liam Darcy was rude to you, and I know he possibly posted that awful video—"

"Possibly?"

"—we don't know it was him. He sure didn't shoot it, as he was featured in it. I can't believe he would post something that shows him in as bad a light as it shows you."

Jane's logic is sound. Okay, I'll begrudgingly forgive him for the video. Still…

"It is incredibly nice of him to invite our family," she continues. "He hardly knows us, and yet he's included us in his dinner party. I think we should be gracious and accept his generous invitation."

By this time, Mum and Lydia have disappeared into the bedroom to plan outfits.

With Jane on board, I have no choice but to submit to the flurry of activity in getting ready for this fancy dinner being hosted by the Darcys. Lydia flashes a string bikini at me.

"Why did you pack a bikini for a holiday in the middle of the Northern Hemisphere winter?"

"We're doing a stopover in California on the way home. It's a bit like the Gold Coast temperature-wise, isn't it?"

"Still too cold for a bikini." I'm not a fan of showing so much skin in public. But Lydia is not me.

"I'm not a Victorian prude like you."

I glare at Lydia. That was harsh.

"This is a formal dinner, Lydia, and it's the middle of winter. Please don't embarrass me by asking to swim."

"Embarrass you? I think you're way past that." She laughs at her pointed observation.

I wince. Surely they won't mention that horrible New Year's Eve dance again. I'm wearing the reminders in the form of color coordinated bruises on my hip and thigh. I don't need any more. "I don't feel very well. I might stay home." Avoid the drama. Avoid the pain.

"Oh, Elissa. Please don't stay home." Jane is dressed in a cute flowery dress over black leggings and boots, and I take a moment to reconsider.

"Stay home if you must, Miss Elissa. Nobody is going to miss you."

Ouch. Does Mum ever hear how nasty she sounds sometimes?

"I'll stay with you, if you like," Dad offers. My father is not the most social person you could ever meet. He's halfway through his new crime-thriller novel and I know he'd love the excuse not to go out to a stranger's house.

To go or not to go. Why was there this urge to go and see Liam Darcy's celebrated home? Especially when he represents all that is wrong with the world—entitled, benefiting off the misery of the poor, environmentally careless, and rude.

"I think I'll stay home with Dad for a quiet evening. I really don't feel well."

Jane's look of concern almost undoes my decision to keep the small lie to myself. I *do* feel unwell—my conscience is at war with some stupid attraction, creating cognitive dissonance. That was bound to make a person feel unwell.

"Perhaps I should stay as well." Jane's words do not match the drooping look on her face.

"No!" Lydia's screeched objection makes my eyes water. "If you and Jane both stay here, I won't be allowed to go."

"Jane," Mum has her most conciliating tone in use, "you can't disappoint your sister. She's got her heart set on this dinner."

Typical Jane. She is torn.

"You will be glad to see Matt." I throw in the sweetener and she is convinced.

"I would like to go." She turns sad eyes in my direction. "But I'd really prefer for you to come as well."

"She will be perfectly fine," Mum says, adding a huff of exasperation. "Now hurry along."

Wow. Mum's obviously already dismissed me as better left at home.

Which elicits deep feelings of perversity. Those same feelings that object to ostentatious displays of wealth and privilege, the same feelings that draw me to fight for environmental causes *and* a tendency to share my unsolicited opinion, which may explain my lack of fake friends. These feelings are guaranteed to make me a barrel of laughs tonight.

"Fine, Jane." I lift my chin and shove a tight smile at my mother. "I'll come."

CHAPTER 6

*W*hy had I ever thought this was a good idea?

My stomach knots as the smell of browning meat wafts through the indoor pool living space. I've given Brenda—our cook who normally would take care of these meals—the night off. I figured barbecue might be easy enough, it being the one thing I feel half-confident to cook. Earlier, Georgia had helped me arrange things to look nice, setting the long table out here with some of that artistic flair she is known for, even though she'd said she was only planning on hanging around long enough to make sure I spoke to Elissa and apologized properly. Gran has insisted on retiring to her room, where she is sure to be watching some British crime show. It's clear she still isn't interested in my guests, but anticipation at seeing Elissa means I don't let it bother me. And while I think the space looks nice, with its lit lanterns and ambiance, and the other guests seemed to approve, I hadn't counted on disappointing the Aussies.

After meeting them at the door, my anticipation soon fizzled, as apart from a quiet hello, Elissa doesn't look at me. Her younger sister also ignores me, while Jane, her older sister, is more gracious, offering thanks for the unexpected invitation, and apologies that they are late due to a miscalculation with their GPS. As I escort them down the hall, the excited murmurs and gleam in Mrs. Bennett's eyes steadily fades as we pass the more formal rooms and continue the long passage to the newer addition at the back. I can't help but notice Elissa's pretty lips have pressed into a flat line, like she disapproves of the antiques handed down through generations.

"And this is where we like to entertain," I say, opening the door to the room that houses the pool and assorted accompanying extras, along with a lounge, barbecue grill and dining areas.

"Oh my gosh!" Lydia's screech could peel paint. "Wow! It's amazing." Lydia hurries to kneel beside the Roman-inspired, dark blue, tile-clad pool, touching the water as if she couldn't wait to dive in.

"I think it's probably a little cool still," I call.

"I don't care. I want to swim."

I glance at her mom, but she's eyeing the surroundings with a drooped mouth. Elissa too seems to be looking around with an ever-increasing frown.

"I can't believe there are chandeliers above the pool," Mrs. Bennett breathes.

Yeah, I'd thought it a little ostentatious when Granddad had first built this room, but some of the sheiks seemed to like it. "It's nice to use it and not have to worry about the weather," I say.

"Oh, to be so rich to not have to worry about the weather," Elissa murmurs. "How much electricity do you use to heat this place?"

I glance at her, and her gaze narrows. Is she ticked off that I'm rich? That I like to be warm when it's minus twenty outside? I feel like explaining this is solar heated and move in her direction, but she inches away to join her sister who is talking to Matt Kennedy.

Before I can follow, Mrs. Bennett accosts me, placing a hand on my arm. "Do you mean to tell me we'll be eating out here?" she asks, pointing to the long stone dining table, the plates and flatware waiting for the meat to finish browning and the guests to take their seats.

"I thought having barbecue out here would be nice," I admit. And keep any screeches away from Gran's ears, her bedroom being on the second level in the front of the house.

"Barbecue?" Her nose wrinkles. "I certainly didn't think we'd be eating sausages when we came here."

Sausages? Oh, right. I remember one of Trinity Lake's relocated Aussies, Peter Franklin, once explaining the difference between an Australian barbecue—what we'd call a grill—and what we call barbecue here. "We don't have sausages. Just some ribs, pulled pork, and salads."

She still looks worried, so I hasten to assure. "I hope you'll enjoy it. And it's pretty nice here. If you look up you'll see the skylights where we can see stars, cloud cover permitting."

Mrs. Bennett glances up to see the ceiling, but her face has settled into petulant lines. I look around. Elissa and Jane are still with the others. Lydia seems to have disappeared.

"And I thought you might find this more relaxed than in the dining room," I offer.

Mrs. Bennett's gaze swerves back to me, her chin rising as she eyes me. "Why?"

Um…

"Do you say that because you think all Australians prefer to have a barbecue than a formal dinner? Or," her voice has risen, "do you mean to imply you thought *we* wouldn't fit in?"

I blink. "That's not it at all," I protest.

"Mum," Elissa hurries over and hushes her, her gaze meeting mine then veering away, her lips compressed.

A disconcerting twist inside suggests it's not hard to see where Elissa's easily offended manner comes from.

"Hmph. And I thought he wanted to make up with you," she says, adding a loud sniff for good measure as she nudges Elissa.

Her daughter's gaze drops, and I feel another twist of regret. I was so relieved she'd come—I might've actually prayed she would—but after an initial hello she's barely spoken to me, instead moving away whenever I draw near, like she's scared I'm going to dump her in the pool.

"I hope you enjoy it anyway," I manage to say stiffly, before moving away. Honestly, Mrs. Bennett would give my grand-mother a run for her money in the candid stakes. Why hadn't I thought this through better? What could I do to help Elissa see I'm not trying to show off, that having people in my home like this is really rare for me?

I return to the kitchen area, another extravagance, but there was something nice about having a summer-type meal in winter. I open the door to the smoker and test the pork. Yep. Juicy, smells delicious, and just needs a few minutes to rest.

I try to look busy and not like I'm Mr. Awkward hiding in the kitchen at his own party while the others play. I'm really starting to regret this decision.

"That smells awesome," Georgia offers, having finally conde-scended to make an appearance.

"You know it." I gather the forks to commence the pulling. "Good to see you here."

"I had to make sure you were doing things properly." Georgia nods to where the others are now congregating around a table of pretzels, cheeses, and dips. "They seem to be having fun."

"Maybe if having fun means being offended," I mutter to my sister's smirk. "I honestly didn't imagine people would think I'm offering a substandard meal by eating out here."

"Really? Who had the nerve—? Oh, let me guess. The mother?"

"Bingo."

"You poor thing."

"I'm pretty sure she resents me for not having footmen serve a sixteen-course meal on the best china in the dining room."

Her chuckle fades as she nods. "Just make sure you get the chance to talk to Elissa, okay?"

"I kind of get the impression she doesn't want anything to do with me," I confess.

"And yet she still came tonight, so it's not a completely hopeless case, is it?"

I guess not.

"Don't make me dare you," she warns.

But my sister's words make me wonder how I can get Elissa alone. Maybe after dinner, when she's feeling more relaxed—which reminds me that I should've probably checked if the bar was fully stocked. I don't drink except when absolutely necessary, but I like my guests to feel like they can. And I've always thought the bar area next to the rattan sofas offers something of a tropical island vibe. Even if I know the Caribbean never gets snow like what's banked up outside the windows now.

"Wow."

I note the conversations have stilled, and follow Georgia's gaze, and my own jaw drops before I quickly avert my eyes. Lydia has obviously found the changing room and swapped her shirt and skirt for an eye-popping tiny bikini.

"Lydia!" Elissa's hiss bounces my attention back to her. "Put some clothes on."

"Why? It's a pool, and I want to swim."

"But—"

"Liam?" Lydia calls. "Is it okay if I have a swim?"

"Uh," I glance at Elissa, whose red-cheeked expression seems to hold more embarrassment than judgement now. But her ducked head means she's still giving me no clues. "Aren't you cold?" I ask Lydia, only half-looking at her.

She lifts one hand above her head and strikes a body-confident pose, like she's readying for a Victoria's Secret gig. "You've warmed this space so nicely," she purrs.

"I think some people here are feeling rather warm," Georgia murmurs.

I'm not one of them, but yeah, it seems some of the other guys don't know where to look.

"Oh, let her swim if she wants to," their mother says.

I clear my throat. "I suppose, if you really want to, you—"

"Thanks!"

Without waiting a second longer, she runs to the pool and with a loud shriek dives in, hurling an enormous splash across the Kennedys and Jackson, who up until now have been watching, open-mouthed, like a horror show. I notice Matt shake his hand dry.

"Wow," Georgia mutters again.

Exactly.

"Good thing Gran isn't here."

So true, I think, as the exhibitionist ducks underwater, releasing the room to relief and soft conversation again.

But it seems we have spoken too soon, as movement at the door draws our attention to our grandmother, who surveys the scene with a wrinkled brow not unlike what I saw on Elissa's face earlier. Actually, scrap that, because a quick glance at Elissa and Jane reveal they're both looking worried again.

But my first duty is to Gran. I hurry over to her. "Gran? I thought you were having a quiet evening upstairs."

"I thought so too," she says. "But it seems some noises can travel."

No guesses which person was responsible for making those noises. The one swimming, or—I frown—not swimming, as the case may be. The one whose shrieks of laughter were even now bouncing off the arched ceiling, as she stood in the water, her arms wrapped around her, covering her front.

"Lydia? What are you doing?" Jane asks.

"Oh my gosh!" Another high-pitched peal of laughter that draws a sigh from the elderly woman beside me. "I can't believe it!"

"Believe what?" Jane asks.

"When I jumped in my bikini top fell off!"

IT CAN'T GET any worse. Surely. This flamboyant stunt must have the Darcys wondering how quickly they can get us out of the house. Lydia is laughing and I feel beads of sweat begin to form on my top lip as I worry about her forgetting to keep her arms strategically placed.

"Where are the change rooms?" Jane has come to stand next to me. Thank goodness she has snapped out of shock into being proactive.

"This way." Georgia Darcy steps by and gestures for us to follow. Bless her. She kindly leads us toward the small change rooms next to the wooden paneled sauna. "There are towels in there. I'll see if I can get the rest of the guests seated and ready for dinner. Hopefully, that will divert their attention."

Georgia moves away with her optimistic plan and Jane goes into the changing room and retrieves a towel. I'm just standing here, frozen. I thought my being flung into the air as a dangerous missile on New Years' Eve was the most humiliating thing ever. I was wrong.

"You go and sit down, Elissa," Jane says as she walks by. "I'll take care of Lydia."

Despite the fact that Mum was doing her best to make a Broadway spectacular of the whole debacle, Georgia has switched from shy wallflower to a commanding host—either that, or the rest of the guests are politely turning away from the Bennett family shame. Was it pity or disgust? Whatever it is, I'm horrified.

"Mum, leave Jane to help Lydia. Come and sit down. It looks like the food is ready to be served."

Thankfully, there is one thing more important to my mother than making ill-informed, loud, and insulting statements—food. The delectable smell of the smoked meat is enough to help her forget that we are not in the formal dining room being served food on silver platters with periwinkles painted on the Royal Doulton china. Georgia's smooth and confident hosting makes me wonder why I had thought she was a recluse. Gary Wickley's opinion possibly has something to do with it.

Eventually, Jane and Lydia take their seats at the table. I can see that Jane is tense. You have to know her really well to see it. To the untrained eye she would look unflappable, but her beautiful smile is forced. She is upset with Lydia's behavior. Even as Matt Kennedy speaks to her with what looks like undying devotion, Jane smiles, but there is worry in her eyes. What will Lydia do next? I can't help but empathize, knowing our sister, and knowing not to expect any support from our mother. It's a good job I'm not trying to impress anybody.

"Thank you for coming, Elissa."

My stomach tenses. Liam Darcy has snuck up on me and taken the recently vacated seat next to me.

"Thank you for the invitation." I want to turn and face him properly, but I'm still struggling with uncertainty. "My family was overwhelmed by your generosity."

"Your family?"

What was that question for? Oh, why am I second-guessing everything? *Answer the man!* "Yes. Lydia was particularly excited to come, as you can see. I'm very sorry for creating such a scene."

"You didn't create a scene."

The generosity of his answer touches me, giving me the confidence to look him directly in the eyes. "I recall not so long ago I created a scene that has made you quite famous on social media."

This time Liam smiles. The chocolate eyes are on the offense again. Good gracious, I could melt.

"I wanted to apologize for all of that." Liam pulls the chair in closer and appears to relax. "I'm not a dancer—ever—but I let Jackson needle me into taking to the floor. It was the worst possible decision, and I'm terribly sorry."

"Given I'm 'okay, but not pretty enough to tempt you'"—why does that still smart?—

"I'm surprised you allowed yourself to be persuaded." Was that awful of me to mention what I should not have heard?

"I'm terribly sorry about that as well. I shouldn't have let Jackson push me into certain things I wasn't ready to do."

"Like dancing?"

"And like admitting I find you attractive."

What? My heart takes a lap around my body and finishes upright and at attention.

"But I do not want to impose," he continues. "I just wanted to apologize. Please forgive me."

I swallow. What can I say? He found me attractive? He's invited my disastrous family to dinner so he can apologize?

"Liam?" His grandmother is calling him from the head of the table. I'd thought she was not going to join us, but she must have found something entertaining about my circus-performing sister and has sat down to the meal. "Come here!" she calls.

And I thought I had problems with my mother.

"Excuse me, please." Another warm smile, and he pushes back his chair.

There is an empty feeling that rushes into the spot he vacates. This is silly. I can't stand the man—can I? Well, he has apologized. I have forgiven him, and now, if only that video can stop trending, we might be able to put the whole sorry business in the past and move on. To a Darcy-less future, I tell myself firmly.

"Do you mind if I sit next to you?"

I'm snapped out of my tumultuous thoughts as Georgia pulls out the vacant chair. It is her house, her table. What did she think I would say?

"Thank you for your kindness just now." I feel obliged to recognize her gracious assistance in calming the Lydia's lost bikini fiasco.

"No problem."

We eat, and I might've moaned a little about the delicious tender pork and ribs. "This is really good."

"Liam's not a bad cook when he gets the chance."

"He made this?"

She nods, her glance stealing to her brother at the head of the table. At his small smile, my heart ripples and I instantly look away.

"It's nice to eat out here," Georgia continues. "I must admit, I love having the pool to use in all seasons. It's relaxing and helps me burn off stress."

"Stress?" I'm fishing for details as to why she hides behind her brother's overbearing façade. There must be a story here.

Georgia shrugs. "You know how it is."

Hoo boy. I know stress, all right. My mother and sister bring my stress measurement scale to heart-attack-high levels most of the time they're around, but I really can't see that Georgia has much in life to be stressed about.

"So how long will your family be staying in Trinity Lakes?"

Georgia is not forthcoming in details about her life, but not shy in finding out about me. I don't begrudge her. She seems to be a pleasant person. "We're here for a couple more days, then I have to get back to my university studies in Seattle."

"Seattle?" Georgia sits up a bit straighter. Is that interest in her eyes?

"Yes, I'm studying a Masters in Environment and Sustainability at Seattle University."

"Wow. That is so awesome. I'm so interested in that sort of thing."

A shame her brother doesn't follow her lead.

"Have you started university – I mean college? I assume you've finished high school."

"I was supposed to go last year, but…"

But what? I want to push, but it's impolite if she doesn't want to share. Was Gary Wickley right? Does Liam restrict her every movement and not allow her to study?

"Anyway, I'd love to hear more about what you've been studying."

Georgia's eagerness is endearing, so I explain a little about my passion for the environment and sustainable practices. Somehow my conversation carries us through the delicious food until dessert. Georgia's questions about some of my stints working with disadvantaged communities around the world sparks memories and reignites my passion for what I do. "Don't you think it insane that there are people in the world who don't have electricity?"

"You sound exactly like—"

Georgia's lips clamp shut, and I wonder who she was about to say.

"Anyway, enough about me. I want to know more about you. What course would you like to study if you could?"

She murmurs something about photography and visual design.

I gesture to a striking framed photograph of dark green hills and a purple-toned river on the wall behind the bar. "Is that one of yours?"

She nods.

"It's really good. I love the colors. Was that taken around here?"

"It was taken at dusk on the ranch in summer. You should come back here and see how pretty it can be."

But returning meant the risk of running into Liam Darcy again, and while seeing the ranch held some appeal, my conflicted feelings toward that man meant it was best to avoid him if I could. There is no point inviting any more trouble. Moving on, remember?

"Do you intend to enroll in a college soon?" I ask, deliberately changing the subject.

"I might, for the next academic year. But..." she bites her lip. "I, um, have been going through some stuff, you know. I, er, just needed a bit of time at home."

I'll bet. It's like Wickley said. Liam keeps her on a fairly short leash, it seems. Poor girl. "If you ever come up to Seattle, come and stay with me. I'd love to show you around campus and talk about what courses might be good to study."

"Oh, would you?" Her eyes light. "That would be so good."

We swap phone numbers.

"Be warned, I'll probably take you up on that."

"Please do. It would be my pleasure."

CHAPTER 7

"And the latest fiscal reports indicate that profits are increasing, but any true measure will need to factor in the counter market forces. We need to be especially mindful of the potential for a shrinking economy, and how that affects our budget for future economic development. And so, unless there are any questions, that concludes page two. Now, if I may turn your attention to page three in your report, I'd like to highlight the regressive—"

I tune out the words. The dry delivery of the Chief Investment Officer does nothing to pique my interest, especially as I've heard it all before. This presentation to the board in Seattle is for their benefit, not mine. Pemberley Enterprises's CIO had given me the highlights earlier. And I hired Max Appleton for his ethics and excellent financial ability and vision. It's not like he's here for entertainment value.

That phrase shudders a memory from last Saturday through me, something Gran said later, when the others had gone.

"Good gracious. Did she think she was part of a cabaret act in Las Vegas? I cannot believe the disrespect. Imagine if anyone had filmed it! The Darcy name would be mud, and you could kiss many of your donors goodbye. Linda Bennett—"

"Lydia," I'd gently inserted.

"I don't care what her name is! That Bennett girl is little more than a classless clown. I don't want you to have anything more to do with that family."

Heat had risen at her request. After exchanging glances with Georgia, I'd protested. "I really don't think you can label everyone in the family like that just because of one person's actions."

"One person? What about that awful mother?"

Okay, two.

Mrs. Bennett hadn't exactly shied away from trying to cozy up to Gran to find out all the gossip about the Darcy family, little realizing that Gran despises gossips and would sooner pierce her tongue than tell a virtual stranger all the family's dirty laundry.

Last Saturday was a complete mess. I clench then flex my hands. On a scale of one to ten that had proved a minus two for good ideas.

I still can't get over it. I feel doomed to disaster wherever Miss Elissa Bennett is concerned. Honestly, the only good thing about that night was seeing the way she and Georgia seemed to click. Everything else—Mrs. Bennett's disagreeableness, Lydia's wardrobe malfunction, Elissa's avoidance of me, Gran's horror at it all—I'd be happy to light a match to my memories and blow it up and all away.

"…and the market indicates that global equity levels being what they are, have the potential to negatively impact the capabilities of…"

As long as it didn't negatively impact what happened in the African water wells project. I might be the biggest anonymous private donor to the Foundation's fundraising efforts, and I'd hike up my contributions to cover any shortfall rather than see those affected by the project do without. Again, the idea stirs to go visit and see the project in person, followed by a random thought to see if Elissa Bennett would want to come. It'd be nice to prove that I'm not the environmental wastrel she seems to think I am.

I internally roll my eyes at myself, sure this morning's rushed breakfast meeting meant I didn't get my two coffee shots like I usually need to function on days with back-to-back meetings. No wonder I'm thinking so weird. I mean, please. Elissa's obviously not enamored with me in the slightest degree, so the opportunity to visit the world's poorest nation is hardly going to appeal. Especially in my company, which she'd made clear she would rather avoid. The whole evening that I'd designed to make things up with her had instead proved to be a gigantic fail on so many levels.

At least I did manage to apologize finally. Not that I'm sure she forgave me completely, but hey, that's up to her. I did my part. But honestly, I'm prepared to overlook her less-than luke-warm response to my apology because of the way she and Georgia seemed to talk for hours. Watching the two of them together, laughing, smiling, made me so thankful. But also a little envious. I'd love to know what they were talking about, but when I later asked Georgia (out of Gran's hearing), she just said it was about college courses. This again spurted pathetic gratitude to Elissa for helping my sister look ahead once more. Then Georgia told me that I really should get to know Elissa, as we had a lot more in common than some people might think.

"Doing my best," I'd mumbled.

"Yeah, your best isn't really working, is it?" Georgia eyed me with that patronizing expression little sisters seem born with. "Sounds like you need help."

"Please." I check out the ceiling and restrain a sigh.

"No, I mean it. She seems nice, and nothing like trashy Cassie at all. Even if her sister…"

"Please, no."

"And you thought I needed to go to a shrink. Can you imagine the field day he'd have with her?"

I don't want to imagine it. I can't tell if Lydia's attention-seeking behavior is a result of personality, lack of parenting, or a desperate cry for help. To be honest, I only have enough care capacity for one teenage girl in my world, the one I share parents with. I can't expend emotional energy I don't have on someone else.

"...and so this proposed transaction, subject to appropriate due diligence and documentation, will enable the business to expand their range and market share in key areas including..."

I hide a yawn behind my hand, as my troubled thoughts return to my sister. Maybe I should see if there is a way of getting her into a course. I contribute enough to several west coast universities that you'd think they'd be willing to help her out. But honestly, just the thought that she's even considering going to study feels like the win of the year. Thank God for Elissa, and her capacity to care.

That thought makes me think I should contact her, maybe see if I can glean some of what she might have said to Georgia. And hey, if such a discussion has to happen over a meal in a nice restaurant, well, I'm not opposed to that. Especially if there's candlelight involved, and—

"Excuse me, Mr. Darcy?"

I straighten, as I realize Max is talking to me. "Uh, yes?"

"What do you think about that proposal?"

For some reason that last word simultaneously makes my skin tingle while memories claw at what my grandmother said at Christmas. She wants me to date, wants me to marry, and to ultimately have kids to pass on the Darcy legacy, although I'm not sure I want to be passing on the Darcy dysfunction. Regardless, that will involve a proposal, to a woman, who my crazy-wild yet stupid imaginings hopes looks like Miss Eliss—

"Sir?" Max holds a frown. "Do you feel okay?"

"Forgive me. It seems I'm not sufficiently caffeinated for this meeting."

There comes a ripple of muffled amusement from several other board members who might be suffering similar challenges, something Max seems aware of as he tosses me a resigned look. I shrug, mouth a sorry, and gesture for him to continue. But mental note: get my PA to send Elissa an invitation to have coffee with me. Maybe we can see if a discussion about my sister can extend to a meal. And maybe even more.

I push back my shoulders and lift my chin. And decisive Darcy is back. I rub my hands. Let's get this done.

ONE LAST DAY in picture-postcard-worthy Trinity Lakes. One last day with Jane, sipping hot chocolate around the log fire at Lakeview Lodge. One last day with Lydia making ridiculous demands and Mum adding lashings of endorsement to ideas like, 'Let's go back to the Darcys' for a swim.' Apart from the winter thing, I've had quite enough of making a spectacle of myself in front of Liam Darcy and his family. On my list of things to do on my last day with my family, revisiting his indoor pool is not one of them.

"Lydia, you can do what you wish on our last day together, but I am going to stay right here by the fire and spend some quality time with Dad and Jane."

"What about me?" Suddenly, Mum wants to be included in all things quiet and cozy. The idea doesn't appeal. "I would have thought your father would want me to get as much sightseeing in as possible."

"I think we've already seen all the sights of Trinity Lakes, my dear." Dad knows how to head her off. "Remember, once we leave here, we won't be seeing Elissa any more during the rest of our travels."

"I don't see why she has to be so difficult. Why can't she come with us to California?"

"My Christmas break is finished," I explain. "I need to get back to lectures in Seattle."

Mum lets out a huff and shakes her head. "You would have thought the Americans would do the sensible thing and run their academic year with the calendar year, like we do."

I don't have the heart to point out that it is quite sensible for them to take the long end-of-academic-year-break over their summer, like we do for our summer, and that our end of academic year coincides with all the Christmas pandemonium. As a consequence, we have school graduation ceremonies mixed up with nativity plays, end-of-school beach parties and end-of-year office parties. All at once. Splitting the chaos into two different seasons actually makes sense, and for me to admit that is something, given I am a staunch Australian patriot.

"Well, you go back to your studies, Miss Elissa, but mind you come back home when you've finished."

Mum stalks out of the room in search of Lydia, who had lost interest in the conversation after the first twenty-three seconds.

"I'm glad you're going to stay in with me." Dad pats my hand. "We can play a game of Canasta."

It's been years since I've played Canasta with Dad, but it is a fond memory. It is just the thing to seal the deal.

"And let's order in some pizza," Dad says. Better and better.

"We're in Trinity Lakes. I'm not so sure they do delivery." Jane hates to upset plans, but she is right. We will have to go out to get some fun food for our last day together.

Lydia has managed to get Mum to let her go out on the town —which is Trinity Lakes' speak for go to the café. I ask them if they will pick up a pizza for us when they come back later. We can survive on hot chocolate until then.

73

Dad, Jane, and I have just settled around our makeshift card table when our whole beautifully planned day at home is shattered. The front door opens and Mum storms back inside. Lydia is trailing behind her. "It's not fair. Why do these things always happen to us?"

"What? What's happened?" Jane's immediate concern is a credit to her kind heart, and contrasts sharply with my annoyance.

"After all these years, your grandfather suddenly decides he needs to move into a care home." Mum waves her phone like a piece of incriminating evidence.

Dad is immediately alert. We only have one grandparent left, Dad's father.

"I thought you said Grandpa would be all right while you were away," I say.

"That's what he told us." Mum has crossed her arms and is glaring at Dad as if this is all his fault.

"I'll call him." Dad moves to get his phone. I can tell he's anxious. "I'm sure Grandpa will be okay for a few extra weeks."

"It wasn't him who called. It was your neighbor." Of course, it was Mum's neighbor as well, but Mum is in full-on blame mode. "Merle said your father has finally lost the plot, and the doctor has suggested he won't be able to go back home."

"We all knew it was coming." Dad sounds resigned—and sad.

"But why now?" Lydia wails. "Can't he stay in the hospital or something for a while? He's had these episodes before. I don't want to go home early."

While Lydia and Mum are making their displeasure known, Jane has already called the hospital back home. It's an international call, and the time zone differences mean it's the wee small hours in South Australia. If Merle has rung in the middle of the night, the situation must be serious.

"I'll put Dad on." Jane hands the phone to Dad and we watch

with concern. By we, I mean Jane and me. Mum is huffing about the house with Lydia whining in her wake.

"I'm sorry, girls." Dad hands Jane's phone back to her. "Grandpa has deteriorated in recent months, but I thought he would be okay for a bit longer."

"What's happened?" I haven't been home for nearly eight months. Last time I saw Grandpa he was fit as a fiddle and saying everything that was outside the new millennium criteria for political correctness.

"He was diagnosed with an aggressive dementia a few months ago. Apparently, it's got so bad he can't be home alone. We're going to have to go back and help shift him into the nursing home."

"I'm not going back yet!" Lydia called from the other room. "I want to finish our trip."

"You can't stay here on your own."

I do a double take. Was that Mum? When has she ever been strict concerning Lydia?

"Jane, you'll have to stay and take care of Lydia."

Aah. And there it is.

"Why don't you both go up to Seattle and stay with Elissa for a few days before heading down to California?"

I open my mouth to object to Mum's suggestion. Jane, yes. Lydia? Spare me.

"That would be such a weight off my mind," Dad says, and I can hear he is genuine. "I can change the flight and accommodation bookings, but I would feel so much happier if I knew they were with you."

Dad rarely asks me for anything, so now that he has, I'm sort of blindsided.

"I don't have room for them in my apartment." My resistance to the idea has been severely undermined, but it is true. I have a paying flat-mate in an apartment that was last rented by a pair of fleas—or people who were not much larger than fleas.

"Let's find an Air BnB apartment near your uni so that you're near school but can still share between times with your sisters."

Crash. That is the falling sound of the last pole holding up my resistance to the plan. I can't say no to Dad.

I look over at Jane and see a sheen of tears has brightened her eyes.

"Oh, all right."

She holds out her arms and Jane comes in for a warm hug. I will enjoy having them with me for just that bit longer.

For several tense moments, I fear Mum is going to insist on staying as well, which is the worst possible idea. Lydia is one thing. Mum is a whole other level of *please, no.*

Thank goodness, Dad has put his foot down—or as close to it as he's likely to come. Mum has no idea how to book flights or change reservations. Dad has made the changes and her loud protestations have nothing to do with it. They are going home to take care of Grandpa. I feel a little sad for Dad.

Our cozy, last day is destroyed. Though Dad can't get flights until tomorrow anyway, Mum is now at home with us, and her lamentations are long and loud.

"Do you want to go out for that pizza?" I ask Jane.

"That would be great."

Escaping the cottage was no mean feat. But Dad was alert to our needs and helped to manipulate the situation to our favor. He promised to take Mum and Lydia shopping in the larger town about a half-hour's drive away, dropping us off for lunch at the Sweet Basil Pizzeria on their way down Main Street.

We found a table in the corner, covered in the obligatory, red-checked table cloth, a candle burning in a jar to add ambiance. The smell of yeasty pizza crust made me feel as if we were going to enjoy good pizza.

"I'm glad we can spend a few more days together," Jane said as she lifted the cheesy slice from the pizza tray.

"Me too." I bite into the cheese and pepperoni pizza and know I've hit the jackpot. "You'll have the worst of it, keeping Lydia out of trouble," I say around a mouthful.

"She's not so bad."

I smile as I wipe my face with a red-checked napkin. Jane's optimism is good for me. Not sure she'll ever convert me, but it's a good challenge.

My mobile phone, that the Americans insist on calling a cell, buzzes on the table next to me. It can't be the rest of the family back from Walla Walla just yet, surely.

"Who is it?" Jane asks.

It's a number I don't recognize, but it's an American number. I'm mildly curious and so begin to read the text.

Hi Elissa,

I hope you don't mind that I asked Georgia for your number.

Georgia? Darcy? My stomach tenses.

I heard you and your family will be leaving Trinity Lakes soon. I've enjoyed getting to know you, despite our mishap at the start. Would you have time to go out for dinner this evening? Just you. I don't think another round with your family would help our getting to know one another, especially given how often our attention is drawn to some antic or other. But I would love the opportunity to see if there is something worth pursuing between you and me.

My mouth falls open. Is he serious?

I have booked Walla Walla's Hattaways on Alder in the hopes you will agree.

The presumption of the man!

I look forward to your reply. Best regards. Liam Darcy.

"Who is it?" Jane has stopped eating and is looking in my direction.

I open and close my mouth several times, the words flying around my brain refusing to land in any sensible order—or in any language that is appropriate to blurt out to Jane.

"What?" The concern is evident in Jane's expression.

"He is the most arrogant person I've ever met," I fume.

"Who?"

"Liam Darcy." I clench my hands.

Jane is silenced, and her eyes search to see if she can read the message still in my hands.

"Here." I shove the phone around for her to see. She takes a few moments to read the text, while I take those moments to practice deep breathing techniques.

"Oh, Elissa. He doesn't mean to be rude."

"Doesn't he?"

"He's asked you out to dinner. He likes you."

"Does he?"

Jane is looking pained.

"You can't say no," she says.

"Can't I?"

Poor Jane. She is pleading a lost case. I should feel some sense of repentance at my jumping to conclusions, but that man…

Honestly. Does he think adding insult to invitation is likely to bring an affirmative?

CHAPTER 8

or real?

I stare at the message on my phone, the words still as ugly as when I first read them a minute earlier. "Unbelievable."

"What's wrong, boss?" Ben Morrow asks from New York, via Zoom.

I shove my phone back in my pocket, the anticipation that had been riding high all day now withering to a pathetic crumbling heap, like the presumptuous person I apparently am. According to Elissa anyway. I try to refocus on the screen, but my head is all kinds of scattered, on the same level as those first few days after I found out what happened to Georgia, but not quite as bad, of course.

"Nothing."

"Uh huh." Ben eyes me a moment longer, then apparently gets the message my raised eyebrows send, and coughs and moves on.

But what he says is a blur, and I try to retain his words and make the expected comments, but I'm afraid it's the proverbial 'in one ear and out the other' and I soon ask him to send me an email detailing the most important points. I have a funny feeling he's already sent something similar through, but I'm not about to let that stop me. I say goodbye and drag out my phone again. Flick it open to where the message still taunts me.

Shot down, is the expression Georgia would likely use. I can think of others that display a similar lack of sensitivity that's reflected in these words. Knifed, disemboweled, slashed open, any pretensions I had carved apart like with a sashimi knife.

She didn't even pretend to be polite with a greeting, just jumped straight in.

Seriously? You booked to go out tonight without even asking me? For future reference, a last-minute invitation doesn't sound too genuine. And I can't believe Georgia gave you my number. FYI: there is no way on earth I would EVER go out with you. Especially when you insult my family. Please do not contact me again.

Ouch.

Well, okay then. I guess that's a no.

I glance out my office window, catching a glimpse of ferries crossing Puget Sound, the grayness of the water matching my mood. I didn't know disappointment could sting like this, like burning tentacles wrapped around a limb that were sure to leave a scar, or maybe require an amputation. And it's stupid that I care so much, but it's been so long since I chased a woman —not arrogance, just stating the truth—that I'd forgotten what rejection tastes like.

Bitter.

I slump back in my leather office chair, allowing myself a minute more to wallow. I have a ton of work to do, and I know I need to get out of this funk. The trouble is, I once heard a self-help guru talk on winning the battle of the mind, and the advice to sit in disappointment, to stay there long enough to learn from mistakes, is something that resonates deep inside.

"I will never, *ever*, do this again," I murmur. I will never ask a woman out again. "Never," I say more firmly, so my ears get the memo too. And especially never dare presume to ask—

Further ruminations dissolve in the James Bond theme song ringtone—unprofessional I know, but GG is always changing it and I haven't had time to change it back—and I realize just who's calling. Great. The person who got me into this mess, with her insistence that this year I do things differently.

I press speaker. "Hi Gran."

"William, how are you?"

I offer the obligatory "Fine." I've learned over the years that nobody really wants to know how you truly are and telling Gran I've just been blown off by one of the Bennett family is not going to help matters there at all. Instead, I listen to her complain about how another storm is predicted soon, and that I really should be careful if planning to travel in my plane.

I bite back my first response, one I might've shared over-zealously in the past, about how I don't appreciate personal calls in the middle of a workday, to which she'd replied, "Then why did you answer the phone, William?"

How to explain I will always put the wishes and welfare of my two surviving relatives above business needs? Except, a snaking thought murmurs, when it came to asking Elissa Bennett out.

Guilt forces me to be patient, to explain the safety measures of my plane are based on factors other than the type of fuel used, but as this is a track of distraction we've gone down many times before, I'm grateful when a beep alerts me to a new call. I glance at it, then grimace, but at least it's a chance to end this one. "Sorry, Gran, I need to take this."

"Okay. We'll talk soon. Love you."

"Love you too," I say, then end this call to get the new. But I've missed it, and when I try again it's busy, and I suspect she's leaving me a voice message. Playing phone tag is so much fun.

Finally, her phone rings through. "Liam!"

"Georgia."

"I just left you a voice message."

Figured.

"So? Has she answered yet?" The upwards inflection in her voice holds hope.

I close my eyes, thankful this is a phone call and not Zoom or Facetime. "Yep."

"And? When are you going out? More importantly, *where* are you going out? I don't think you should take her to a dinky little diner. I mean, Joe's Diner is nice and all, but she's classier than that, and it's not like there are too many options in Trinity Lakes, unless you go to the country club. But even there you're so well known that you'll probably be harassed by people wanting you to invest in their schemes."

I grind my teeth, wishing I hadn't told my sister the plan. The price of getting the phone number for a scorpion.

"Liam?"

"Yeah, looks like it's a no."

There's a beat of silence. Two. Three. "She turned you down?"

Her tone sounds piqued, or maybe that's wishful thinking, as the next minute I hear a low whistle followed by a, "Wow."

Right? Thank you, Georgia.

"What on earth did you say to her?" she asks.

Huh? "What do you mean?"

"No woman in her right mind would turn you down, so it has to be something you said to her."

"I didn't say anything bad," I protest.

"Read me the message you sent to her," she commands.

"Georgia—"

"Do it."

She's kinda scary sometimes, my sister. But maybe it would help to have a female perspective. So I read what I'd written, and I'm taken aback when she makes a sound that's suspiciously like a giggle.

"What?" I ask, irritated.

"Oh, poor Liam. You're not very good at this, are you?"

"Apparently not," I mutter.

"It was the comment about her family."

"Well, yeah." I spill what Elissa wrote back to me, which gets me a gasp, and the sudden panicked feeling that makes me wish this was a video call so I could see her. "What is it?"

"It's *my* fault. I shouldn't have given you her number."

"Come on, GG. I don't think that's true."

"Um, didn't you hear what she said? Oh," her voice is quiet, all earlier amusement drained away. "I feel so bad now."

I clench my hands so hard my knuckles go white. I hate that my actions have caused my sister pain. I know I can't protect her forever, but with all she's gone through, I don't want her to experience any more trouble. So the fact I've made her second guess herself, just when she'd started resuming the sassy confidence I'd always loved about her, makes me feel even worse than when that stupid message first arrived.

"It's my fault, Georgia, so don't blame yourself, okay?"

I hear a sigh.

"Okay?" I press.

"Fine," she mumbles, before releasing another sigh. "I really thought we'd clicked, and never in a million years thought she disliked you so much."

"Appearances can be deceptive," I offer, feeling the fullness of that lame response.

"But Elissa *is* different," she insists, and I know it's true.

Elissa Bennett might have the manners of a barracuda, but there is something else there, a loyalty to her family that I appreciate and understand, and the fact she's not impressed by money or looks is refreshing to me. And honestly, after years of being chased by scores of predatory women, I'm kind of drawn to being the one who has to make the effort. For I feel she is a prize worth having, her passion and quick wit even more appealing than her looks.

"I might have to message her," Georgia says.

"Better you than me."

"Yeah. Hey, I'm sorry, bro."

"No biggie."

I rub my forehead, wondering at myself for using words like biggie, when Georgia's voice comes again.

"I'll message her now." I hear faint taps, like she's writing as we speak.

"Oh, but—"

"Too late." Her voice holds a smirk, as I hear a *swoosh* that suggests words are now flying through cyberspace.

"What did you say?" I ask, despising myself for caring so much I want to wheedle out details from my sister.

"I just apologized to her for sharing your number, said I'd talked to you, and that you were devastated—"

"You did not!"

"No," she says slowly. "But maybe I should."

"Georgia," I warn, using my best older-brother tone.

"Oh, it's so cute the way you think I listen to what you say."

I hear a faint *ping*, and then Georgia's, "Ooh!"

I chew my lip, not wanting to enquire, even though everything inside me demands to know if it's Elissa. Oh, hang it. "Well?"

"Well what?" she says innocently.

Really, the best thing I could do right now is to hang up the phone. Except if I did that I know I'd be wondering all afternoon. And the work piled up on my desk would be ten feet deep still.

"Poor man," she says, taking way too much delight in pitying me. "So, do you want to know if it's from Elissa?"

"Yes," I grit out.

"Well, it is."

I close my eyes, dig deep for patience. "Okay."

"Do you want to know what she said?"

"I really have some work to—"

She laughs. "She said *No harm done*."

"Did she?"

"Yep." She exhales loudly. "Well, I guess that's something. I'm going to reply and see if she's still able to meet me in Seattle next week like we planned."

"Right. Okay. Well, I really should go," I say.

"Yeah. Maybe I can come see you if you're still in Seattle when I visit."

"I'd like that, but I have a meeting in DC this weekend, so we might need to play it by ear."

"Sure."

We say our *love you's* and goodbyes, and I hang up, my mind spinning over what she just shared. While I'm glad I haven't wrecked the burgeoning relationship between my sister and the one woman she seems to regard as a friend, I can't help but gnaw on Elissa's words, which I know are untrue.

No harm done?

Maybe not for her. But for me...

THE CHILLY BITE of the wind seems to match the ice that is freezing through my veins. We hadn't been gone from the pizza bar two minutes before the words of my reply text began to reverberate in my mind. I need to get back to Lakeview Lodge, to the warmth where I can think straight.

"Am I a terrible person?" I lay my head on Jane's shoulder the moment we get back inside, closing out the cold wind behind the cottage door.

She twists the ring on her finger. "Of course not."

Jane's answer is predictable, but is it true? She pats my cheek like a parent who is encouraging their downcast child. But that's the point. I think I may have acted childishly. "I am, Jane. I'm a terrible person."

"Why would you say that?"

I open my phone to the text message app and hand it to her. As she reads, I can see that tiny little frown form, which confirms my assessment. I am the worst.

"See?" I have a small hope that she will still fight for my innocence, but instead, she lifts soulful blue eyes to me. I drop my head in shame. "I was too harsh, wasn't I?"

Jane lets out a long sigh. This is worse than I thought. I've never known Jane to give me such a lecture. And she's barely said a word.

"What should I do?" I am suddenly overcome with remorse.

"He has been so kind to us, Elissa. I don't know why you dislike him so much."

To be honest, I'm not quite sure why either—now—on this side of having pressed send.

"Why didn't you stop me?"

Jane's expression deteriorates another two degrees. This is a positive roasting.

"You think I'm like Lydia, don't you?"

"Lydia is young and impetuous."

"So it's *worse* than that. You're saying I should have grown up by now. Oh, Jane. Why didn't you tell me?"

A dreadful thought hits me right between the eyes. Now I'm in blaming mode—like Mum. I throw myself on the couch as self-awareness taps me on the shoulder and shakes its finger of disappointment my way. I *should* have more self-control. I *shouldn't* be so quickly offended. And I definitely shouldn't be blaming Jane.

"I'm so awful!"

Jane responds to my lament by coming and sitting near me.

She kindly runs her hands through my hair, something that has always been so soothing.

"You show your good heart by being able to admit your faults."

I fling myself upright and look Jane straight in the face. "Jane, I love you. You are the best sister in the world, but you are too gracious to me. I think perhaps I deserve just a small scolding."

"Your actions have their own natural consequences. I hope you will learn and grow through this experience."

How is it my sister sounds so wise, like she's lived a hundred lifetimes, yet she's only two years older than me?

My phone, still in my hand, pings. My mouth dries. Is this Liam sending back a nasty text in response to my harsh rejection? I can't look at it and hand it to Jane.

"It's from Georgia."

"Oh, no. He's told Georgia." My heart sinks to my kneecaps.

"She's really sorry to have shared your number with her brother."

An icy wash swishes through my stomach and up to my chest. I didn't think about how Georgia would respond, because, of course Liam would share it with her. I didn't think about how Liam would respond. I just didn't think. Jane is right. My actions have their own natural consequences, which I am experiencing now. I feel awful.

No harm done.

I press send and flick the text away.

"Elissa. You should stop and consider first before sending off a text."

Jane is at the height of her reproaches. She is right. She is one hundred percent, absolutely right. I resent Mum because of her thoughtless ways, I criticize Lydia because of her impetuousness, and yet in terms of thoughtless and impetuous actions, I believe I've won the gold-medal. I put my head in my hands. Grow up, Elissa. It's way past time to practice maturity.

I hear the front door slam. Apparently it's also time to put my hard-learned lesson into practice. Mum, Dad, and Lydia are back from their shopping spree, and I need to tone down my judgement a solid ninety percent.

"I thought you were going to wait for us to pick you up," Lydia said, the moment she walked through the door.

"It is only a ten-minute walk, and the weather was fine." By fine, I mean it wasn't snowing or blowing a gale. It was cold enough to make my toes numb, and bite my face in all the exposed places, but I needed those physical discomforts to keep my mind from my bad behavior.

"How was the shopping?" Jane asked.

"Hopeless." Lydia flung herself on the couch next to Jane. "You'd think for all the cute shops they have here I'd find something, but nope, not a thing."

Several harsh thoughts launch, but my own self-reproach shoots them down. Hard-learned lessons that felt so bad had to have some use.

"I'm pretty sure you'll like the shopping in Seattle. I know of a number of great outlets." Did my positive cheer sound forced? It was a bit, but I am trying to be a reformed woman.

"Well, all we need to do now is to have everything packed and ready for an early morning departure." Dad had sat in the recliner near the fire. "We need to get to Spokane airport before eight for a ten o'clock flight. Are you sure you're happy to drive the rental car back to Seattle and drop it back at the office there, Elissa?"

I haven't done a lot of driving in the US in the seven months I've been here. Driving on the opposite side of the road and taking exits and negotiating smaller roads are going to take my full concentration, but I know Jane will help me keep focus.

The late afternoon before our final meal together in Trinity

Lakes is busy as we pack and tidy, getting ready to leave. I'm beginning to miss Mum and Dad already. I know Mum's crazy, but she is my crazy. And Dad is my rock. He's not loud or demanding, or judgmental or rude. He's also not highly sociable, but he is steady and reliable. I give him a hug as he puts the large suitcase by the front door ready for tomorrow's departure.

"What was that for?" he asked.

"Thanks for coming to spend Christmas with me. It's been great having you all here."

Typical Dad has little to say in return but wraps me in a warm hug.

By the time everyone has settled in their beds for the night, I am still wide awake and restless. It is only nine p.m., but Dad is adamant we must be ready to depart by six-thirty. He's one of those 'better to aim for half an hour early, so if you're late, you'll be right on time' kind of people. However, during the Christmas break, I've gotten used to keeping much later hours. Besides, my conscience is rattling around inside my head, and refuses to leave me alone.

No harm done.

It was a thoughtless statement. If Liam had told Georgia what I'd written, and because they were close he would have, then harm *was* done. Georgia would be feeling rotten about having shared my phone number. And, I guess, Liam probably feels rotten too. It's not nice being rejected at the best of times— let alone with words as sharp as the ones I'd tossed out. Thoughtless, impetuous, nasty.

"Oh, fine." Jane stirs as I give in to my nagging Jiminy Cricket. I don't want to wake her, so I take out my phone and pull the cover over my head, like a teenager still reading after lights-out.

Hi Georgia. I'm sorry for what I sent to your brother this after-noon. I know you care for him a great deal. I hope you'll forgive me. If it's still okay with you, I'm really looking forward to you coming up to

Seattle and us getting together for some shopping, maybe a spa day or something fun. Let me know when you're free. I'm attaching a screen shot of my lecture timetable so hopefully we can coordinate a day. Let me know. Elissa.

Jiminy Cricket gives me a pat on the head and flies away. At least now I can get some sleep.

The phone pings before I put it back on the bedside table.

I can't wait! I'll get back to you with dates. G.

CHAPTER 9

I peer out the plane's window and see the blue-green water and the green-brown of the islands just off the mainland. A moment ago we'd passed over Mt Rainier and the snowy caps of other mountains, those markers that remind us we're almost there. As much as I enjoy visiting the nation's capital, there's something to be said for heading west again knowing I'm heading into a slightly more relaxed environment. And while some might consider Seattle to be a big city, compared to others I've visited—London and Tokyo come to mind—it's still quite small in the whole grand scheme of things. But I like the hills, I like the proximity to water, and the islands that hold the hope of escape. Puget Sound reminds me a little of Sydney Harbour, and there's a way more relaxed vibe than what I experience on the east coast. Maybe it's because I know I'm closer to being home.

I straighten my papers as the plane tilts and begins its descent, and Marco reminds my fellow passengers of the need to stay buckled up. This might be my plane, but we've decided it's more environmentally and economically efficient to offer it as a private plane on occasion, so there are certain times when

I'm travelling long distances when we accept other passengers. I let Marco take care of that, and the retired United pilot is happy with the arrangement. It works out better for me, as I hate the cringe-inducing optics of being known to heavily invest in environmental causes and yet I have my own plane. But at least this plane runs on biofuel—recycled cooking oil—something that surprises most people when they learn about it.

An hour later I'm being driven to another meeting at the Grand Hyatt, this one about a scheme to support women in Mexico. Ever since what happened to Maria, our former house-keeper, I've become more acutely aware of the mistreatment of women, and the femicide that occurs in and around Mexico City means I'm wanting to do what I can to alleviate some of the pain. Not that anything can ever make up for the loss of life, but at least if honest police can be resourced to catch the—

"Sir, we're here."

"Thanks." I give the driver a twenty-dollar tip and exit the cab, entering the lobby as a bunch of men wearing the colors of Calgary's hockey team are followed by burly suit-wearing men holding coffee cups. Probably here to play at the Climate Pledge Arena. I have box seats—one of the perks of being a major sponsor—and I want to catch a game, but business hasn't really allowed for much fun. I wince at memories of the failed Mr. Fun, and how my sister dared me to squeeze a bit more joy out of life. Well, I tried. And look how well that turned out...

"Mr. Darcy?" One of the receptionists has a big, red-lipsticked smile. "Your suite is ready."

"The usual?"

"Yes, sir."

I take the room card she offers and motion to my bags, and she assures me someone will bring them up immediately. I thank her and head to the elevator.

My suite has floor-to-ceiling windows that offer glimpses of Elliot Bay and I take a moment to admire the view sandwiched between two high-rises. I've got an hour or so before I meet the Mexico representative, who's fitting me in before travelling to meet officials in Vancouver. I wonder about my sister again.

Her last message was a little cryptic, and I'm not sure where things remain between Elissa and myself. But at least it sounds slightly better than before.

She apologized to me for what she said to you.

Hey, I'll take it. Not sure if that makes me a special brand of pathetic, but something is better than nothing, right?

I pull out my phone and shoot Georgia a quick message. *Hope you're doing okay. I'm in Seattle, and there's a spare bed if you want to come hang out. We could catch a hockey game if you want.*

I'm not exactly sure that watching a hockey game is any kind of inducement, but I'm willing to negotiate if it means it gets her here to the city. There's plenty of other things we could do, and if I know my sister she would be excited about the opportunity to take photos of fresh scenes. So maybe—

My phone buzzes with a new message.

We're here, just three blocks away. How funny is that?

I type back *Who's we?*

A second later, a new message. *Me and Elissa and her sisters.*

I blink. Rub my eyes. It's been a huge day, having gotten up early then crossing the entire continent. Had I misread that? But the words remain the same. Elissa was here. With Georgia. And her sisters. And while I didn't mind Jane, I had no great desire to see the youngest Bennett again. As for seeing Elissa, my tense stomach isn't sure that's such a good idea. And it's not like she'd like being blindsided by my sister and her interference.

Um, why are you all here?

Her reply takes a little longer to come. *Meet us for dinner and you'll find out.*

My heart kicks, and I know a real urge to do just that, but my responsibilities swarm to the fore. *I can't,* I type. *I have a meeting.*

Of course you do. Eyeroll emoji. *Spoilsport.* Three seconds later it's followed by, *I dare you to blow it off and come.*

I quickly tap, *It's for the Mexican women's femicide project I told you about.*

Oh. Smiley face with a halo emoji. *You better go to that then.*

I chew my lip. *Maybe after? How long are you here for anyway?*

Her reply is swift. *The weekend.*

Huh. Anticipation tingles. Well, it's only Friday afternoon. Who knows what the night could bring?

GEORGIA IS A LOAD OF FUN. Jane has taken Lydia shopping while Georgia and I indulge in a day spa.

"Let's get a makeover." Georgia is enthusiastic.

I'm reluctant to rain on her parade, but I'm at the end of my budget for extravagances.

"My treat." It's as if Georgia has read my mind. "My brother has been nagging me to get out and have some fun for months."

"You don't do this as a regular thing?" I know the Darcys have the money and can definitely afford it.

Georgia goes quiet. Something is wrong, and a moment of worry threatens to swamp me. But she takes a deep breath in and out through her nose. She wants to tell me something. I don't know how I know, but I do. I don't say anything else but wait.

"Something happened—nearly a year ago now—and I've kind of, you know, been reluctant to leave home."

I want to ask what happened. My imagination rushes about trying to make guesses based on limited clues, and though I come up with several alarming options, I don't dare to voice any of them.

"This is the first time I've had the confidence to come out." She smiles shyly at me.

"Well, I'm glad." I pause. Will she give me more detail, or should I just pretend I have no interest and move on?

"So I know that Liam will be more than happy to fund my little day of spontaneous activity."

I'm a little stuck for words. Spontaneity is not my usual method of operation and taking money from Liam Darcy doesn't sit well with my pride either.

"Please, Elissa. Nothing too dramatic. We've had a facial, let's just get our hair done, nails and makeup, and buy something nice to go out for dinner tonight."

The sadness that had briefly appeared on Georgia's face flashes through my mind. She's been in some sort of self-imposed seclusion for nearly a year.

"If you're worried about Liam, don't. I have my own account to spend as I want. I'm not usually a frivolous spender, but this sounds like fun."

"I tell you what, if you skip the manicure, I'll do it."

"Skip the manicure? Why?"

I hold up my hands with my very sensibly clipped finger-nails. My days of playing sport and the guitar have been my excuse to avoid the glamour of fake, colored nails. Georgia grins and holds up her fingernails as if for a netball pre-game inspection.

"I've never done nails either, but I thought it might be fun."

"Can we skip it this time?"

"Sure." She reaches out and squeezes me in an excited hug. "I like that you said, 'this time.'"

Huh. So I had.

"So, new dress first and then hair?"

How can I say no?

Several hours later, I take stock of our busy day. It has been fun, and I'm at our Air BnB apartment dressed up to go out on the town.

"Do you want us to come too?" Lydia has a few shopping

bags dumped on the living room floor, but is dressed in jeans and a sweater, with a stocking cap over her long hair.

"Oh, Lydia." Jane speaks up. "I had my heart set on staying in with take-out and a good movie. Won't you stay with me?"

Lydia blinks, surprisingly speechless. I blink. What is that offer all about? I mean, it does make it easier for me, in the sense that I would feel obliged to pay for Lydia and Jane if they came, and it is an expensive restaurant. But I would do it if they want to come. Lydia obviously does, but Jane has this other scheme. And it sounds like a scheme. I wonder what she's up to.

"She's expecting a call from Matt Kennedy," Lydia says. "I suppose I can stay with you, Jane. I'm hoping for a call as well."

"Who from?" I can't help asking. I know that Jane has a thing for Matt, but who has Lydia managed to exchange phone numbers with?

"Never you mind. You look hot, Elissa. Go out and don't worry about me. You never know who you might end up coming home with."

"I'll be coming home with Georgia, if you don't mind, and will thank you not to imply anything else."

Lydia laughs it off, as usual. I raise my eyebrows in Jane's direction. She gives me a reassuring smile. She will watch Lydia while I'm out.

Georgia has talked me into wearing heels and a slinky red dress, with a slit up the side that goes above the knee. I was tempted to get a needle and cotton and sew the slit up, but then I would be hobbled as badly as if I was in a potato sack race. Besides, I feel special, and after we hand off our heavy coats to the concierge, I sense the eyes of more than one person—male people specifically—follow our path to the table near the back of the restaurant.

"You look gorgeous, Elissa," Georgia says as the waiter pushes her chair in.

"Thank you. You look lovely yourself."

"I asked Liam to join us tonight."

I nearly choke on the mouthful of water I have just taken and lift my gaze to Georgia. She is laughing at me.

"Relax. He's not coming."

I swallow the water, hoping that none has come out in dribble or spit.

"Can I ask you a question?" Georgia has me in her sights and I sense I'm in for an interrogation. "Why do you dislike Liam so much?"

Suddenly, I'm embarrassed that Georgia has observed my dreadful behavior toward her brother.

"I know he insulted you at the dance, and then threw you onto the floor."

"I realize that was an accident."

"He's always been shy, and he told me Jackson was pushing him to admit something that he wasn't sure about. Liam thinks you're beautiful."

"Georgia, you shouldn't say things like that."

"Why not? It's true."

"Well, that's nice of you to say, but after the way I've treated him, he must have decided I'm way more trouble than I'm worth."

"He really wants to impress you."

I raise my eyebrows. I like Georgia, but I don't think she understands how passionate I am about sustainable environmental practices. Money does not impress me, especially when it is used indiscriminately without thought to the damage it may do to the future of the planet. And if what Gary Wickley told me is true, Liam Darcy doesn't treat his workers very well either. He is good-looking, I'll concede that point, but I'm not going to tell Georgia.

"If you gave him a chance, I'm sure you'd like him."

"Let's not talk about your brother right now." I pick up a menu and pretend intense focus. The dishes are all listed in Italian. I love Italian food, but I prefer them to be listed in the usual way—Spaghetti, Hawaiian Pizza, Garlic Bread. Fancy words like Polo and Carne and Insalata and Quattro Formaggia only confuse me, but I need to stay focused and choose something. I want to avoid talking about Liam Darcy.

"I know you're not impressed by wealth, but perhaps you don't realize how generous Liam is."

"People with loads of money can afford to be generous. It's really the least they can do."

It takes a few moments before I notice Georgia has gone quiet. I look up and she is staring at her menu, worrying her lip with her teeth. I quickly review my last statement. Sometimes I can be an insensitive clod.

"I'm sorry, Georgia. That was unkind of me to speak like that. I'm sure your brother is generous. Please forgive me."

"He doesn't just give money, Elissa. He gives himself. He couldn't come tonight because he's attending a meeting to address the issue of femicide in Mexico."

I frown. It sounds serious but I have no idea what it means.

"The high number of women killed by violence whose murders remain unsolved. Our housekeeper had a sister who was killed by her husband who was never charged. Since then Liam has added this to his list of causes he donates to."

Wait. He has a *list* of causes?

"Prevention of femicide is something that needs awareness and strategy the world over."

I can't disagree with that. But I'm surprised to hear that Liam has gone to support the cause in person.

Georgia closes her cloth-covered menu with a snap. "Anyway, I'm having the gnocchi with Gorgonzola cheese sauce and sprinkled with beetroot shavings."

I have no idea what that is, but it sounds fascinating.

"Can you translate the menu for me and order something that is similar to pasta with red sauce."

Georgia laughs. Thank goodness. She's forgiven me.

The food is next level in terms of flavor and presentation. Definitely a step up from Pizza Hut. The waiter keeps bringing more bottles of imported mineral water when the one before has only a little left. Fancy bubbly water that probably costs as much as the wine. But I've never been a wine drinker. In theory it looks like it should taste lovely and sweet, but in my short experience of wine tasting, I've always found it tastes... I can't explain it, but it's not sweet. So I've skipped the wine.

"Are you going to order dessert?" Georgia asks as the waiter clears the dishes from the table.

I'm a sweet tooth. I thought that dessert was a given. But then, this new dress that started out snug is definitely feeling a little tight around the middle at the moment.

"Perhaps we could share a dessert?" I ask hopefully.

"Possibly." Georgia looks at the dessert menu. I should say, *Dolce* menu.

She looks up and smiles. Wait a minute. She's not smiling at me but looking at someone behind. I have a moment of panic. Please. Not now.

"Liam," she says, and my worst fears are confirmed. "You're just in time to split a dessert with Elissa."

CHAPTER 10

I swallow. Then have to swallow again. Okay, I'd thought Elissa Bennett was pretty before, but now... I don't think I've seen a more beautiful woman ever. And certainly none I've wanted to make a good impression on as much as I do right now.

"Liam? Put your tongue back in."

What? I snap to and straighten, shooting a look at my sister, whose smirk says she's teasing and I've not embarrassed myself too much just yet. Plenty of time for that still.

"Hello, Elissa," I say, holding out my hand. She places her soft palm in mine, which sends tingles racing up my arm. "I hope my sister hasn't been too annoying today."

"Not too annoying, no." Her mouth curves. "Actually, not annoying at all. We've had a great day."

I smile, drinking in the perfection of her skin, the way her cheeks hold a special glow, the sparkly depths of her eyes, the plumpness of her bottom lip, the way that candlelight seems trapped within her hair.

"Um, Mr. Darcy?"

"Liam," I correct.

"Could you please release my hand?"

Oh. I let go, but instead of her snatching her hand back and wiping it, like I suspect she would've done a week ago, her gaze holds tentative entreaty, like she feels as unsure as me. Which fuels fresh hope that maybe—

"Um, hello? Brother dear?"

I tug my gaze away from Elissa and wrap my smirky sister in a hug. "You."

"You can thank me later," she murmurs, in a voice Elissa hopefully hasn't heard.

"Sir?" A waiter hovers nearby. "Will you be joining these ladies?"

"Yes," Georgia says, gesturing for me to take the seat facing the window next to Elissa.

I lower myself obediently, and a dessert menu is placed in front of me.

"I'll just give you a few moments," the waiter says, before disappearing.

I slowly exhale, and force my attention to the page, and not the woman seated at right-angles to me. It might be winter outside but the woman is hot, hot, hot. And I'm conscious I need to talk, to explain why I'm here, to find out why she's here *sans* sisters—for which I'm enormously grateful—and to—

"How did your meeting go?" Elissa asks me instead.

"My meeting? Oh." I glance at GG who nods subtly. So she told Elissa. My gaze returns to Elissa. "It went well. These issues are deep-rooted, and change doesn't happen overnight, but we're hopeful that with time we'll see progress made."

"I've never heard of femicide before," she admits, her eyes on me, making me feel like I'm a solo act in an ice-skating spectacular. One false move and it's over.

"Did Georgia mention about our former housekeeper?"

A dip of the golden-brown head.

"She had to leave us when her sister was killed and return to

Mexico to take care of her nieces and nephews. She was adamant it was her brother-in-law who had done it, and we couldn't believe the police never closed her case. Well, they have now—Luis was charged last year, thanks to the efforts of a new woman-led detective squad we support, but it's awful to think that people get away with it just because of their gender."

Her blue eyes have widened, are luminous in the candlelight.

"But you probably don't need to hear me talking about something so gritty and—"

"I asked, remember? And I think it's a good cause. An important cause," Elissa says. "I…I admire you."

Her validation soaks in like butter on hot toast. It's kind of weird being successful. I'm often surrounded by people who offer sycophantic praise and adulation, or who feel like I hear it all the time so I don't need any more encouragement. So to hear words of affirmation from someone who's not been shy about her criticism means I can trust her words as gospel. Elissa's words, like Gran's and my sister's, are honest.

"And what have we decided here?"

Elissa's soft smile drifts up to the waiter, and I'm caught by the elegance of her throat. She's so classy. So—

"Liam!"

My sister's hiss draws my attention back to the waiter again.

"Sir?"

"Sorry. What was the question?"

"The young lady wishes to know—"

"Do you want to share a dessert with Elissa?" my sister cuts in.

"Uh, sure?" I cut a look at Elissa, who eyes me uncertainly. "You don't want your own?"

She shrugs and offers a small smile. "I'm not really very hungry, but I've seen some of the desserts others are eating and they all look so good."

I nod. I'm not much of a dessert eater, but if it gives me more time with Elissa, then I'll order every dessert. Which makes me turn back to the waiter. "Do you have a dessert sample plate?"

"Uh—"

"Would you ask the chef to make a dessert sample plate? Tell him I'll make it worth his while."

"I can ask," the man says.

He leaves, and I notice that Elissa is eyeing me uncertainly again. Did that just seem too arrogant? I don't like splashing the cash but if it gets the job done...

Maybe change the focus. "So, what did you two get up to today?"

GG gestures for Elissa to take the lead, so I listen to the soft accent I'm growing increasingly fond of. I feel like I'm learning Elissa, with everything from her intonations to the way she sometimes talks with her hands, her non-ring wearing, non-painted fingernailed hands. Unpretentious. What you saw was what you got. Real. Honest. Authentic. I'm liking this woman more and more, and sure don't need any sugary confections for the rush of sweetness I'm feeling now.

"And how long are your sisters staying for?"

She explains about her parents needing to return to help out her grandfather, and again I'm caught by the compassion evident in her tone, the sheen in her eyes.

"It's hard, isn't it, when you lose family."

"I know it's inevitable, especially when people get old, but I'm still feeling bad that I'm here and not there." She toys with her water glass. "I can do video calls, but it's not quite the same."

"No."

I shoot another look at Georgia, who subtly points at her friend, as if wanting me to talk with Elissa some more. Okay, then. "So, uh, I was wondering—"

"Sir?" The waiter of awesome timing has returned. "I thought I'd let you know the chef is prepared to make an exception tonight and is happy to make the dessert sampler."

"Excellent."

The waiter looks between us. "So will that be for two or three?"

"Oh, two," Georgia says, holding up a hand. "I swear I couldn't fit another thing in."

I could swear that my sister was looking for any reason to leave us alone. God bless her.

"In fact," she says now, as the waiter leaves again, yawning then patting her mouth. "I wonder, Elissa, if you'd mind terribly much if I excuse myself to powder my nose."

"Oh, I'll come too."

Wait, that wasn't supposed to happen. Was it just the usual bathroom twin thing women seemed to do, or was it something I said?

I tell myself not to be insecure and stand to help Elissa pull out her seat. She seems surprised by this, but how can I not be a gentleman, especially when she's dressed like that?

I return to my seat as the women leave, and I'm almost glad as it gives me the opportunity to appreciate Elissa's dress anew. She didn't seem the type for red, or slits, but both really worked for her.

"Liam Darcy?"

A new voice draws my attention to a passing diner, and I look up to see a business associate from Portland. We talk shop for a few minutes then I'm aware that Elissa is returning. And honestly, I'd be prepared to lose a million dollars rather than lose a moment with this woman. "Excuse me."

He nods and moves away, and I stand and pull out Elissa's chair. Gran would be proud, although it seems I've flustered Elissa again. "Where's GG?" I ask once I've resumed my seat.

"GG? Oh, Georgia? She said she'd be out in a moment."

I nod. "So, you've had fun today?"

She smiles, and the look of ease returns to her face. "I like your sister."

"And she likes you. She doesn't have too many female friends, so the fact you've taken an interest in her really means a lot. Thank you."

The color on her cheeks deepens to a darker rose.

"What are you up to tomorrow?" I ask, wondering if she'd be up for extra company.

"Um, I hadn't really thought about it too much."

"I guess you've done some of the touristy things. You know, seen Pike Place market and the Space Needle."

Her smile is wry. "Lydia kept pestering me, but I've been busy with my studies."

"Can you tell me about what you're studying?"

She nods, then shares about her coursework, her focus on environmental issues and sustainability another check in her favor. I'm honestly kind of amazed at how what she's studying syncs so well with what the foundation stands for. I wish she could join Pemberley's research team.

"You should come out to the ranch again, see what we do there."

She sips her water again. "Why?"

"We have some innovative sustainability practices you might be interested in. Things that look at water conservation, soil management, and the like."

"Really?" Her mouth ticks up. "From what I've seen, Washington state doesn't exactly have a problem with a lack of water. Not like from where I'm from, anyway."

"Would you tell me more about that?"

As she describes living on the land, I'm drawn into her vivid descriptions of drought-affected farms, animals being put down, farmers shooting their stock—and themselves—due to the harsh conditions. I barely notice that our dessert has been served, intrigued by the passion and compassion she shows, especially when she reveals one of the main reasons she started studying was when a school friend's father took his life due to years of unrelenting hardship. "Which of course did not make things any easier for his family." She shakes her head. "Anyway, I'm determined to do whatever I can to help our planet. And I'm sure that we can manage farms in more sustainable ways."

"I agree."

The way her eyes hold mine, coupled with her small smile, seems to hold a wavering kind of kinship, something I'm ready to dive into and explore. But then I'm conscious that Georgia is nowhere to be found. My chest tightens. "Um, how long did Georgia say she'd be?"

"Oh!" She blinks, as if, like me, she's only just realized my sister isn't here. "Um, certainly not this long." She pushes back her chair. "I'll go check."

"Wait." I touch her arm, and again that rush of sensation tingles up my skin. "Check your phone."

She does, and I check mine. And sure enough, there's a message from my sister.

You're welcome.

I release a huff, and glance up to see Elissa is holding a similar expression. "What does yours say?"

"She apologized and said she needs to go back to the apartment because she's feeling tired. You'd think she just would've come and said something." Her forehead wrinkles.

Sometimes I really love my sister. "So I guess it's just you and me."

She bites her lip, and again I'm attacked by another bout of insecurity. "I can take you back if you want. Or call a cab. Or—"

"I don't mind staying a little longer," she says, her voice, her eyes shy.

"Neither do I. I'm really enjoying getting to know you more," I add in a stupid burst of honesty.

"Me too," she says softly.

Courage emboldens me to say, "Do you think your sisters

would mind if I took you all on a tour of Seattle sites tomorrow?"

She bites her lip, drawing my attention, and it's like my eyes can't move past her mouth. What would her kiss be like?

"I can ask them. But don't you have work or something to do?"

"Not this weekend," I say firmly. I'll clear my schedule.

"That could be nice."

The soft voice holds a lilt, like she's actually looking forward to it, which fuels courage for more. "And if you were free the following weekend, I'd love to show you the ranch. We could go horse-riding if you're into that kind of thing."

Her smile flashes. "I grew up on a farm. What do you think?"

"I think, yes?"

She laughs and nods, and I feel like fist-pumping myself because I finally made her laugh. "Let's make a date, then."

Her eyes widen, and I almost backtrack, but then decide I don't want to deny the fact I want to date her. Dating her is a yes from me for so many reasons.

I'M FIGHTING with the dissonance that is nagging me. I've agreed to go down to Trinity Lakes for the weekend. I believe the word 'date' was used in the original invitation, and my curious heart is packing a bag and indulging in delicious anticipation. However, my over-developed sense of integrity is furiously pointing out a breach of ethics. Previously, I've made loud and self-righteous statements about decreasing our carbon footprint —and Lydia knows it. I'm trying to head her off at the pass by examining my own hypocrisy in this situation.

Liam Darcy has offered to take me back to Trinity Lakes in his private jet. Oh, the conundrum. It's no use me postulating and making dramatic ethical statements like: I'd rather take the bus. Apart from the fact I don't have eight hours to take the bus as I've only got the two days free, I really want to go to visit the Darcys again. Not to put too fine a point on it, I really want to get to know Liam more. He is a strange contradiction.

Tall, dark, handsome, rich. He is all these things, and I dismissed him out of hand for his arrogance, entitlement, and environmental insensitivity. Apart from the private jet thing, I seem to have been wrong. Tall, dark, and handsome seems to be translating into highly desirable, and his being rich is highly convenient for the purposes of a quick flight to make the most of the weekend. Of course, I'm not going to mention any of this to Jane in case Lydia overhears.

"Don't forget to pack your bathers." Lydia grins at me as I put my hairdryer into the small travel case. I ignore her. I also don't bother to mention I have them tucked at the bottom just in case swimming comes onto the agenda.

"What are you and Jane going to do this weekend?"

"I thought you knew." Lydia flops onto my bed. I stop and search her expression.

"Matt and Lucy Kennedy are coming up for the weekend. We're going to go out to the Space Needle, as it's listed as the number one tourist spot on Google. Jane wants to go to the Pioneer Square Historic District, but I think I'll pass."

"Don't make her go on her own, Lydia. You know how Jane loves historical things."

"Who said anything about her going alone? Matt will take her."

I have a million questions, but I'm not certain that Lydia is the person to discuss things with.

"She's in love with him." Lydia answers one of my questions without me asking.

"How do you know?"

Lydia taps her nose. "I might not have been to university like you two clever ducks, but I know love when I see it."

"Do you?" I wonder what she sees in my future.

"Like Liam Darcy is madly in love with you."

I freeze. Is he? Can she read minds? Why does she think that? Oh, I'm so not ready for this conversation.

"What are you going to do while Jane goes out with Matt?" I ask instead.

"I'm hoping Lucy will go clubbing with me."

"Lydia."

"Stop fussing, Elissa. I'm nearly nineteen. I'm more street wise than you know."

"That's what I'm afraid of."

"Relax. Lucy will be with me. What can go wrong?"

"Lydia, please don't do anything silly. Lucy might not be into night life."

"Just make sure *you* don't do anything silly." Lydia throws my advice back in my face. "Going off in a fancy jet with an older man."

"He's not that old. And how did you know about the jet?"

"He's bringing Matt and Lucy here from Trinity Lakes and taking them back again first thing Monday morning. It's not what you know…"

Honestly, nothing gets by Lydia. I'm suddenly worried about leaving Jane to handle her. But it's too late as there is a knock at the apartment door. Before I can even get to the living room, Jane has answered the door and the sound of voices indicates that Matt and Lucy have arrived. This probably also means Liam has arrived to pick me up. A full swarm of butterflies let loose in my stomach and proceed to fly up into my chest, then down into my intestines. This is ridiculous. I'm a grown woman, not an overgrown teenager like Lydia.

I zip up my bag and place it by the bedroom door, then walk calmly out into the crowded living room. Despite the noise and the crowd, everything else in the room suspends into silence as I zero in on Liam. He's standing just inside the door and our gazes meet and lock. I'm not sure I'm even breathing anymore. Then the moment is broken when Lydia snaps her fingers in front of my eyes and laughs. "Yep. You're a goner."

The noise comes back into my consciousness, and I realize I must have looked like a stunned mullet. I test out a smile in Liam's direction. He must've been waiting for my cue, as his face breaks into a warm and inviting smile, the laugh-lines around his eyes and mouth bringing life and hope into my heart. Good grief! I *am* a goner. I have to pull myself together.

"Just give me a couple of minutes, Liam," I call over the hubbub in his direction.

He gives a small wave in return.

I know I've said a perfunctory 'hello' to the Kennedys, kissed Jane goodbye, given the usual 'mind-how-you-go' lecture to Lydia and picked up my bag, but it has all been performed on autopilot. There was no sincerity in any of it. All I can think of is getting to Liam's side and out the door. There is a sudden attraction that must have grown steadily over last weekend's time together—somewhere between catching the hockey game together, and the relaxed meals we shared, my feelings have gone from zero to hero. All that keeps me from complete abandon is to think of all the carbon-heavy fuel we will be using to fly back to Trinity Lakes. That thought, and only that thought, is what keeps me in some semblance of dignified order. If not for that unforgivable sin I could possibly turn into boy-crazy Lydia, except with the boy-crazy dialed up to one hundred.

CHAPTER 11

Somewhere between the private airstrip and the stables
I lost Elissa. I don't mean I actually lost her, but she
grew very quiet, the nervy questions on the plane about the
places we were flying over fading, as the enormity of what was
happening seemed to dawn. As we landed it dawned on me, too,
as I realized this was the first time I'd invited a woman home
since Cassie. And the feelings I'd had for her were nothing like
those I held for Elissa now. And it seemed by her quietness
Elissa might feel the same.

This might be just a weekend, but it feels like the start of so
much more. Earlier this week Gran had been unimpressed that
my 'friend for the weekend' was a Bennett, but Georgia had
taken great delight in reminding Gran that she'd wanted me to
date, so shouldn't she be glad Liam was doing something about
it? Georgia was thrilled, and I hoped the time away from Elissa's
sisters might allow her to talk more with Elissa. Even if my
guest's conversation had dried up around me.

She'd been polite enough with Gran and Georgia in the
house earlier, overlooking Gran's lack of warmth as GG gave
her a hug, then told us to scoot on down to the stables. I'd been

happy to oblige, and had earlier requested our horses be prepared, thankful the lack of ice or wind meant we could still get our ride in.

I glance at Elissa now as she rubs Apple's nose, the mare instantly drawn to her, or at least the sugar in her hand. "She likes you."

"She's beautiful." Elissa strokes the bay's meticulously groomed neck. "My horse at home is more spirited. This one seems so gentle."

"Don't let first impressions fool you." Her gaze lifts to mine. "I've often found they're not reliable."

"Me too," she murmurs.

There is a kind of magic in this moment, here in the dim shadows of the stable complex. A kind of sweet affinity flows between us, where all I'm conscious of is the trace of waterlilies above the smell of hay and horse, the way a shaft of weak wintry sunlight dapples her face, the way she moves, the sound as she clears her throat.

"So, um, is Apple Georgia's horse?"

My guts tense, and I breathe it away. "Georgia doesn't ride her much anymore."

"Oh? Why's that?"

I still, swallow, wondering how much I should admit. It's actually Georgia's story to tell, but I sense she wouldn't mind me telling Elissa some of the details and spare her the repeated pain.

"Let's mount up and I'll tell you soon. But before you do, I have something for you." I retrieve a wrapped package from a shelf and hand it to her.

She looks at me questioningly and I gesture for her to unwrap it. Her breath draws in as she spies a pair of soft leather gloves.

"It's deerskin lined with polar fleece. I figured you might not be used to riding in snow."

Her smile lights her face. "I'm actually pretty excited. I've never ridden in snow before. Thank you."

"You're welcome. We're lucky it's not been too heavy lately, but it'll still be way colder than you're used to, so I figured those might help." I eye the jeans that hug her legs nicely, and her vest and purple quilted jacket that look like it should keep her warm as well. "Do you want a leg up?" Elissa has ridden in the past. I know she's capable of putting her foot in the stirrup and hoisting herself up to throw her other leg over the saddle, but the temptation to stand close is a good excuse to offer. She smiles in my direction, as if she knows it's a farce.

"Why not?" She gathers her reins in her newly gloved hands, takes hold of the pommel and cantle, and bends her left leg at the knee. "I haven't ridden in over nine months and my leg muscles would probably have me hopping around like a one-legged pirate."

I laugh and take hold of her left ankle to lift. She knows what she's doing as she easily senses the rhythm and moves with my lift, throwing her right leg over the saddle.

"Thanks."

Her statement snaps me out of the frozen state I'm in, and I gather Archer's reins and mount up unaided.

Twenty minutes later we're moving down the trail that takes us to the experimental part of the ranch. This is my favorite part of the estate, with its gently rolling hills leading to greater inclines, sandwiched as we are here between the Cascades and the foothills of the Rockies.

"This is beautiful," she says, pulling Apple to a halt. Her chest rises as she takes in a deep breath of sharp air. "You can really breathe here."

"I love it," I confess.

"I can see why." She glances around, drinking in the land-scape. "Wow."

"Anything like home?"

She laughs and throws me a wry look. "Apart from the fact there is snow, and the trees are like Christmas trees all glistening in the sun?"

"What is the landscape like back where you're from?"

"There is a range of mountains that make up the Flinders Ranges, but not mountains like you have here. And the trees are Australian bush—gums, wattles, acacia. It gets green in the winter, but at this time of the year it is hot and dry."

"It can get dry here too," I say.

"Really? No."

"We might not have the droughts you're used to, but we still can experience water issues."

"But you have so much water here."

"Excessive water withdrawals have put our water resources under stress. It's why I'm interested in water conservation and permaculture—exploring ways we can do better to live more sustainably."

She bites her lip, nods, and looks away.

I take the moment to admire the view. It's obvious she's comfortable in the saddle and there's a new ease about her, which suggests the rest of the day won't be filled with the awkward silences of before. I hope so, anyway.

"What's that building over there?" she asks, pointing to a large structure half a mile away.

"That's the barn we use for the equipment for the dual-use solar project."

"You do that here? I knew about the one in Minnesota, but you do that here as well?"

I nod, heart pinging with pride at her look of esteem. "When my grandfather died this was all ranch land, just cattle, hills, and grass. But I didn't want to do the same, so I started investigating alternative ways of ranching."

I nudge my horse to resume our walk until we're closer to

where the solar panels are positioned in several level fields beyond the barn. Five acres of metal and glass rows that capture the sun, beneath which lay long grasses and wildflowers and grazing sheep.

"I convinced my grandmother that I could turn a profit on this," I continue, "so I invested my own money into my half of the land and explored several renewable energy sources. We hit upon solar as that's something that works especially well in so many developing nations. And then I learned about dual-solar projects."

"It's a win-win, isn't it?" she says, her face alight once more. "Clean energy and protecting ecosystems."

"Exactly. The land used for the production of solar energy is grazed by appropriate livestock, which is why we use sheep instead of more cattle. And the growth of indigenous plants helps preserve the flora, fauna, and ecosystems, all of which helps improve pollination, wildlife, and water quality."

"That's fantastic."

"I love that we're seeing a reduction in both herbicide use and fire fuels, but we also have a more supportive environment for bees."

She nods. "People underestimate how important bees are."

We're nearing the first bank of solar structures, and can now see some of the sheep and, away in the distance, a row of white beehives.

"This all comes under the banner of Pemberley Sustainable Research."

"What?" Elissa looks at me with a frown.

"Pemberley Sustainable Research. Pemberley Green Foundation and Pemberley Holdings."

"That's you?" She looks shocked.

I nod slowly, not sure if admitting to it is the right answer.

"I've heard about it in my research at university. Pemberley Sustainable Research funds huge programs trying to improve agricultural practices around the world, particularly in the developing world."

I actually know this information, but nod, still uncertain of her response.

"That's brilliant, Liam. I'm so glad."

Glad? Well, that's good.

We talk more about the goals of the Pemberley Holdings and the Pemberley Green Foundation, how the ultimate goal is to aid those in poorer countries with sustainable efforts which will help them.

She nods. "I've gone on some trips to southeast Asia exploring how the principles of permaculture can benefit poorer communities. This feels like a natural fit."

Natural fit. It seems increasingly clear that's what Elissa and I were. "I agree."

"I'm really impressed," she says. "I love what you're doing here."

My heart glows. It seems we're on the same wavelength about so many things.

"We've also installed LED lighting that faces downward, which stops light pollution at night."

"I imagine that stops predators from eating the insects you need for pollination," she says.

"Exactly, while also providing benefits for nocturnal animals. Or people who like to look at stars."

"Are you someone who likes to look at the stars?" she asks.

"When I get the chance. When I'm with the right person who appreciates such things."

Is that a blush on her cheeks? I'm still learning this woman, but I think it just might be a blush. Which means she just might appreciate stargazing too.

"We're lucky it's a clear day today, which means tonight should be great for watching stars." Subtle it ain't. But I love the idea of snuggling while stargazing.

A gnawing feeling in my stomach makes me aware that it's been a while since we snacked on the plane. I check my watch, and sure enough, it's way past lunchtime, so this needs rectifying, asap. "Would you like to see more now or would you prefer to grab something to eat?"

I hear a small growl and judging from the reddened cheeks figure it's Elissa's empty stomach saying hello. "So that's a yes?"

"Please. But I'll need to get changed first."

"Your room has an ensuite bathroom so you can clean up as you like."

I nudge Archer into a canter. "Let's race back."

Elissa is a good rider and has got Apple near to a flat-out gallop before I know what's happening. Apparently, she's also competitive. We arrive back at the stables at an even finish. She's laughing, and the cold has her face glowing.

"Thanks for the ride, Liam." Elissa pats Apple's neck and hands the reins to our groom. "It's been too long since I've had some serious outdoor exercise."

I hand Archer's reins to the groom as well and walk back with Elissa to the house.

I've put her in the best room of the guest wing, the eight bedrooms above the pool with views that sweep across the hills. I walk her up the main stairs and turn left, instead of right to the family's rooms. We walk to the end of the hall and wait outside her room. I lean a hand against the doorframe as she twists the doorknob and moves inside.

"Thanks again for a fun morning." Her eyes are sparkling.

"You're welcome. Anytime." The word surprises me as much as it seems to surprise her, but I mean it. "I've loved getting to know you, feeling like you understand me and what we do here more."

"You're certainly not what I first thought."

"And what was that?" I dare.

I think coy is the word for the expression she's wearing now.

"Someone arrogant, entitled, handsome, yet with a great need for reassurance."

Ouch. I'll take the handsome, but the rest... "But now?" I ask hopefully.

She takes a step closer, her gaze traveling up my chest, lingering on my mouth—or is that just wishful thinking?—before finally meeting my eyes. "Now, I think you're kind, compassionate, handsome—"

Her smile pools sunshine in my chest. "And?"

"Still needing reassurance, apparently."

I chuckle. "You sure don't make it easy to impress."

A beat passes as she stares at me. She licks her bottom lip. "Do you want to impress me?"

Admit the truth and possibly scare her? But this woman never shied from honesty, so I finally admit, "Yes."

As her blue eyes widen, that feeling of weighty expectation falls between us again. I sense that if I was to lean in a little more she might not move away, and that maybe I could finally know the taste of her lips.

"I like you, Elissa Bennett. More than anyone else for a long time." Or ever.

I lower my head and lift a hand to trace the soft contours of her cheek. Her breath hitches, but her gaze remains unwavering.

"Mr. Darcy," she whispers.

"Miss Bennett," I murmur, leaning closer—

"Liam? Oh!"

My sister's exclamation snaps me upright and away, her giggle one of the most annoying sounds I've ever heard. "What?"

"Don't snap at me, brother dear. Gran just wanted you to know lunch is ready."

"Great."

"Hey, Elissa, maybe after lunch you and Liam should check out the pool," Georgia says, raising her eyebrows suggestively.

I turn my back on her, sure my face must be as bright red as Elissa's. "Did you bring a swimsuit?"

Her little nod draws new warmth.

"Then in that case, maybe we will."

I'M NOT an exhibitionist like my younger sister. I've brought one-piece bathers. It's surprisingly modest in the world of swimsuits since there's more value for money in terms of material used. Despite this, I'm not exactly brimming with confidence.

"Will you join us for a swim, Georgia?" I ask as we get up from the lunch table.

"Perhaps." She gives me a wink. She won't. Her attempts at matchmaking are as subtle as a brick, almost as subtle as her grandmother's thinly disguised dislike, which is to say, not at all.

"I don't know what's wrong with you millennials." Mrs. Darcy folds her linen napkin up and places it neatly on her empty plate. "When I was your age, swimming was a summer pursuit. It's snowing outside."

"Which is why we have a heated indoor pool." Georgia is not going to be dissuaded from organizing this activity, pushing as hard for it as her grandmother is pushing against it. And I would lay my last dollar that neither of them would appear for the aquatic exercise. I'm suddenly quite anxious.

"Come on, Elissa. Let's go get ready." Georgia heads toward the door.

Liam stands up from the table as well. Is he uncomfortable about swimming—well, not about swimming—that's not uncomfortable. Appearing half-naked takes a load of self-assurance I'm not sure I have.

Georgia has the bull by the horns, so to speak, and leads me upstairs. "I'll come with you," she says. "I could use a nice relax in the hot tub."

It did sound nice, as long as Georgia was there as my buffer.

Georgia may have seemed shy and retiring when I first met her, but she is really quite mischievous. The hot tub is fantastic, and we are sitting enjoying the warm bubbling jets when Liam comes into the pool area.

My goodness. No man has the right to look like that. He is wearing boardies and a t-shirt, and his long muscular legs are not tanned, not surprising in the middle of winter, but are evenly covered with dark leg hair.

"Is the water nice?" he calls across.

"It's great." And that is no lie. The water is nice, and the view from where I'm sitting is pretty nice, too.

Liam pulls his t-shirt over his head. Better and better. Still no tan. Obviously, he's not the vain sort to head to a solarium or get a fake tan. I'm glad. I hate pretension. But tan or no tan, he must work out as his biceps, and triceps, and all the other muscles whose names I cannot remember, are in fine form. There's a stupid lump in my throat, and my mouth has gone dry. I mentally shake my head at myself. I am not a child. A drooling groupie, maybe, but not a child.

Liam has hardly settled in the tub when Georgia launches out of the water.

"I think my phone is ringing. Be back in a second."

She grabs her towel and disappears up the stairs into the house. She won't be back.

I chance a look in Liam's direction, and it appears he is tentatively looking in mine.

"She thinks she's being subtle." Liam smiles.

"I know. I hope you're okay with..." I wave a hand between us.

"Are you kidding? This," he waves his hand between us in the same way, "is something I want to investigate further."

"By investigation, you mean?" I'm almost shocked at my boldness. I know exactly what he means.

He doesn't answer but moves around close enough to take my hand in his. "From the moment I first saw you, I thought you were so pretty."

"That wasn't quite how it sounded when you were talking to Jackson."

"I know. I was embarrassed and wasn't ready to vocalize how I felt. I'd only just seen you for the first time."

"And my family."

"Elissa."

I stop and watch his face. His Adam's apple moves up and down with a swallow.

"Can I kiss you?"

I nod, and he doesn't wait for me to formulate a witty answer—thank goodness—but moves in and touches my lips with his own. It's delicious—and awkward, sitting side-by-side. He senses it too, and stands up, and as he still has hold of my hand, lifts me up to stand with him, the water bubbling around our middles.

"Come on."

What? I thought he was going to kiss me again right there. But no. He has another plan. A better plan. We dive from the edge of the tub into the water, which is relatively cool. I swim to the surface and see him freestyle to be right next to me. Awkwardness seems to have left with Georgia, and I easily come into his embrace, and from there my arms go around his neck, while his slip around my waist. It's a good job we can both touch the bottom, or we would drown. I think I'm drowning anyway—as our bodies merge and our mouths explore each other. Wow. I'm just going to stop thinking. I'm about to sink to the bottom of the ocean called Liam Darcy when I am abruptly jolted back to the present. A voice over the sound system.

"Phone call, Liam. It's urgent."

Liam brings his hands to either side of my head and dives in for another kiss. A quick one this time.

"Wasn't that your Gran?" I'm so breathless I can hardly get the question out.

"She's probably been keeping an eye on us through the security system."

"You mean there are security cameras here?"

He points to three different positions in the area, and I can see those intrusive eyes glaring at us, exposing all my secrets. At least, I had hoped this was secret, just between Liam and me.

"I'm sorry." He kisses me again, quickly. "Gran can access the cameras at any time, but nobody ever does, unless they're worried about something."

"She's obviously worried about you."

Liam swims away and I feel bereft, so I swim after him to the pool steps.

"Let's go somewhere Gran can't keep an eye on us, shall we?"

I hesitate just a moment. Alone with Liam. That sounds lovely, but I'm not sure I'm ready to be so alone that ...

"You look worried."

I open my mouth. How to say what I'm thinking.

"I was just thinking of heading out later for a little star gazing."

"Star gazing?" I can do star gazing. With it so cold out, we will need to be bundled up warm. I need this space. This time. Perhaps I'm a little old fashioned, but I'm not the jump-into-bed-at-the-first-opportunity kind of girl. I'm more of a stable relationship, engagement, marriage kind of girl. "Yes, star gazing sounds brilliant."

I need to wash the salt out of my hair and dry it if I am going to go outdoors in this weather. Liam goes to attend to his 'phone call' and I head upstairs to get dry and rugged up in something warm.

Half an hour later, I'm surprised how dark it is outside

already. I tug my scarf closer as I exit the guest room, and nearly bump into Georgia.

"Are you ready for dinner?"

"Didn't we just eat?" Although, now she mentions it, I'm pretty hungry again. Must be from all that exercise from before.

After another delicious meal, where I do my best to fend off Grandma Darcy's pointed comments about my lack of appropriate social connections, I'm relieved when Liam says he's made arrangements outside, and we finally say goodnight to his grandmother.

"Where are you going?" The disappointment on Georgia's face is priceless.

"We're going star gazing. Want to come?"

A smile lit her face, then she performed a little cough. "I can't. I'm sorry. Maybe I'm coming down with something."

I laugh. Her approval is fortifying in the face of Grandma Darcy's disapproval.

"I'm sensing tension with your Gran." I broach the subject as Liam rolls out a thick sleeping bag in the back of his truck. I throw a couple of pillows up and wait for him to take my hand and haul me up to join him. He doesn't answer until we've made ourselves cozy, snuggled in each other's arms.

"I don't know why she's so antsy. It was her idea in the first place." He places a kiss on my temple.

"What do you mean?"

"She's been pushing me to find a...girlfriend for ages. She, uh...wants me to keep the family growing for future generations."

I feel a surge of heat and stiffen.

"Oh, Elissa. I'm sorry. That sounded wrong, didn't it?"

"You think?"

"I'll be frank. She wants me to find a wife."

"But not an Australian," I say slowly, "and certainly not a Bennett?"

He didn't answer.

"Liam?"

"If you must know, my asking you out may have started with Gran insisting I find someone, and Georgia setting her heart on you, but I have my own ideas about my life."

"And what do those ideas amount to?" I have withdrawn a bit. It's my weakness of taking offense so quickly. I bite my tongue and wait for Liam to answer.

"I would like to get married and start a family, but…"

"But?"

"Elissa, don't let this spoil our weekend. I just want to get to know you, and—"

"And…?"

"And see if there's something between us that is worth pursuing. For the record, I think there is. I think you're incredible."

I think he is kind of incredible too, but this whole hunt for a wife and mother of his children has offended my feminist sensibilities.

We're silent for a few minutes, watching the night sky, as my feelings refuse to settle.

"I promised I was going to tell you about Georgia." He's changed the subject.

I am still slightly withdrawn, but I nod.

"She's about the same age as your younger sister, Lydia. About a year and a half ago, when she was only just eighteen, one of my workmen formed a relationship with her."

"Gary Wickley?"

My eyes have adjusted to the starlight, and I can make out his nod in the dim light.

"And he isn't good enough for your family?"

Liam turns on his side to face me. Even in the darkness, I can sense the intensity in his gaze.

"He got her to go to Vegas with him. Told her he wanted to marry her."

I'm frowning, though I suppose he can't see it. Marriage yes, but to an eighteen-year-old? And a tacky Elvis wedding when she is from such a prominent family?

"Georgia is part owner of Pemberley Holdings. He's highly manipulative, and once she agreed to go, he became quite violent toward her, making threats if she didn't do what he wanted."

"Gary Wickley?"

"I know he tried to charm you and your family. He's a real charmer when he wants to be, but he was after Georgia's money."

"And you stopped it?"

"Of course. What do you think? He's a jerk, and you can ask Georgia, if you don't believe me."

I recall the accusations that Gary had made against Liam. It was the complete opposite to the story I am hearing now. But in all honesty, I had never liked Gary's slick schmoozing. I am more inclined to believe Liam.

Our star-gazing excursion should have been perfect, but my withdrawal, and then Liam's defensiveness when he talked about Wickley, took the shine off the connection we'd formed in the pool.

We came inside after only an hour and said a polite goodnight to each other. Our interaction in the pool had raised longings but the discussion in the cold night had damped those longings down. It's disappointing. I'd thought there might have been something worth pursuing there. Now I'm not sure.

I only take a few minutes to change from my winter woolies into my love-heart themed pajamas. I can't stop thinking of Liam and begin examining my reactions to his Gran's suggestion that he find a wife. Do I want to be a wife? Maybe, depends. Do I want to be Liam's wife? That's a whole different question. And to be fair, he wasn't actually proposing, just filling me in on his grandmother's machinations. Do I want him to propose? I'm thinking, yes. But have I stuffed it up by being touchy? I pull back the soft quilt and am just about to get into bed when there is a knock on the door. Instead of calling out, I go over to see who it is.

"I'm sorry, Elissa." Liam is standing in the hall, a shadow in his gorgeous eyes.

"No, I'm sorry. I shouldn't be so sensitive about things, and I should learn to talk about things instead of letting an idea control my responses."

"Do you want to talk now?"

"Not really."

Liam dropped his eyes and pressed his lips together.

"I'd rather do this."

I open the door fully and throw my arms around his neck. It doesn't take much for him to zero in on my lips, just as I intended.

"Does this clear things up?" I whisper in his ear.

"Very much."

CHAPTER 12

I've had the best weekend. I gently squeeze Elissa's hand as we make the short flight back to Seattle. She has her studies to resume, and I have a big meeting tomorrow before a quick trip to LA, but we've already made plans for next weekend. That thought sparks anticipation, and another that Valentine's Day is coming soon, and I should think of doing something special for her. Because everything about this weekend has already confirmed what I thought I knew. Elissa Bennett is someone special. Someone very special indeed.

My thumb caresses the back of her hand, and from the way her breath catches, I swear she feels the same tingly feelings I do. My mind flicks back to today's kisses in the hot tub, which fortunately Gran was not privy to, as she'd gone to church in Trinity Lakes. Just to make sure I switched off the cameras in that portion of the house, too. I barely slept last night, excitement and something that felt like sheer joy bubbling up for hours as I thought about my time with Elissa. Hugging, kissing, laughing, talking for hours about all kinds of things.

A Sunday morning ride to visit the more traditional part of the ranch only confirmed she knew the ins and outs of managing farm life, as she wrangled gates and made intelligent observations about the livestock and fields. Even the way she handled Gran proved her to have poise and grace one mightn't have expected when first meeting her family. But then, I guess the fact my grandmother has her own sharp tongue that requires tact and care proves that the Bennetts are not the only ones challenged in certain social environments. And they don't have the benefit of America's finest education.

I smile and Elissa nudges my shoulder. "What are you looking happy about?"

"You," I say, and sure enough, she blushes.

Even this modesty is something I love about her. Elissa's one-piece swimsuit might cover way more than Cassie would ever wish, but I like the fact she has the confidence to be herself. And the woman I've grown to know more deeply in these past two days is whip smart yet unassuming, sweet yet holding fire in her eyes and lips. Yeah, Valentine's Day will need to be extra special.

Her grip tightens. "I've had a lot of fun. But there's something I still need to know."

"What's that?"

"I still can't quite understand how someone who is so concerned about the environment can have a private plane."

"Ah." I see it now, the tension she wears in her brow, like there's a piece of the puzzle missing. "It's really proved far more convenient than if I had to rely on commercial flights any time I needed to get somewhere. Saves me hours."

"But it still seems so incongruous with what you're about."

I love that she recognizes what I'm about and isn't afraid to call me out on it.

I face her a little more fully. "This plane has been converted to run on recycled cooking oil."

Her lips part. "Really?"

I nod, then she flings herself at me—or at least tries to, but the seatbelt gets in the way as she releases a squawk.

"Are you okay?"

She hurriedly unclasps the strap and slides across onto my lap, wrapping her arms around my neck. "Everything *is* okay now."

Then she kisses me, and I'm soon lost in a moment of passion that makes me wish we could—

"Ahem, sir?"

Elissa stills, pulls back, as Marco's voice comes over the intercom again.

"You, er, may wish for your guest to return to her seat and strap in, as we're beginning our descent."

"You have video cameras in here too?" she mutters, hurriedly resuming her place, embarrassment shimmering off her like a solar panel's radiant waves in the height of summer.

"I forgot." Her cheeks look as red as mine feel. "I, uh, didn't expect you to get so excited about used cooking oil," I try to joke.

She winces, and I really wish we could go back to where we were ten minutes ago.

I try to cover the awkwardness now floating between us by pointing out through the window some of the city's landmarks lit up in the early evening.

"See all those lights over there? That's where they make the Boeing planes." I point to the city. "That's the Space Needle, and that big square down there is the Climate Pledge Arena where they play hockey. We could maybe catch another game sometime if you like."

"Uh, sure."

I notice she's biting her lip again. "We don't have to if you don't want."

She shakes her head. "It's not that."

"Then...?"

A small sigh. "I just can't help thinking about how all of this"
—she gestures between me and her—"is really nice, but I'm
going back to Australia in June, so what then?"

"In June?"

She nods, her glance veering back to the window. "My visa
allows for this year of study, and my work back home in Sydney
means they're expecting me to return at the start of July."

Why hadn't I realized this? My brain starts whirring, exploring, and chasing down possibilities like I do in the business
world. "So we'll find you a job here."

Her brow furrows. "It's not as simple as that. There needs to
be work visas, and I can't just quit my job. I have signed a
contract with them there, and—"

"We can make this work," I assure.

"Can we?" she asks, once more getting to the heart of the
matter with a few swift blows.

"We can make this work," I repeat, looking her firmly in the
eye, willing her to believe me. For I'm not about to let this
woman depart my life, depart Georgia's life. Not without a
fight. "Trust me."

Her eyes hold uncertainty, then she exhales, gives a tiny nod,
and slumps back against the leather seat. She offers me a small
smile and turns to look out the window as we circle down for
the airport where my plane can land.

But my mind keeps humming. If she's worried that a work
visa can be hard to arrange, then maybe I could investigate
another study option. Maybe then she could explain that she'd
been offered a fellowship or a similar continued research
opportunity. Maybe I could speak to one of those colleges I
support and see if a donation might help pave the way for a new
'scholarship' opening. Which reminds me—

"When did you say you and Georgia were going to look at
colleges?"

"Sometime in the next few weeks."

I settle back in my seat and thread my fingers through hers as the cabin lights dim. "I really appreciate you taking time for her like this."

Her smile holds sincerity and light. "Georgia is special. And not," she taps my chest, "just because she seems determined to put us together."

Together. "I like that word."

"Which word?"

"Together."

I hear her breath catch, and I hope it's in a good way. I know it might seem like a rush, and hey, if you're like Gran and looking at a calendar, well, maybe it is. But there's something about this woman that makes me feel more secure, like she sees me as the man I can be. The man I want to be. And I can't lose that. "We'll make this work," I promise.

"I'd like that," she says.

We're still staring at each other as the plane's wheels touch down, and I don't let go of her hand until the plane has finished its taxiing and Marco informs us over the loudspeaker that we're now safe to undo our seat belts.

Half an hour later we're pulling up outside her apartment complex. I'd love to keep her all night, but with Monday's big meeting with potential investors for the African project, I need to get a good sleep and do some preparation. So, knowing this will be the last time I have her to myself in relative privacy, we annoy the cab driver by kissing in the back seat, until I've almost lost my breath.

"Want me to take you two to a hotel?" the guy asks.

Elissa is fanning herself, looking like she's trying not to laugh.

"That won't be necessary," I say. Maybe I should get my bags out as well and find a different driver. But that's just hassle I don't want. "Are you happy to stay a little longer while I escort my girlfriend upstairs?"

"Your dime," the man says, popping the trunk.

"Girlfriend?" Elissa whispers.

It's a word I've never really used before. Cassie wasn't really my friend so much as offering diversion in other ways. But with Elissa I feel I've found a friend I regard as more. Way more. Like, maybe one day, permanently more.

"Yes." I smile, pleased to see the look of wonder in her expression. "We're making it work, remember?"

She nods like she's willing to believe me, and I retrieve her bags and follow her inside and up the stairs. It's only two flights and then we're there, outside her door, and I really don't want to have to say goodbye. I don't want to have to share her, which I know sounds a little stalker-like, but I feel like her family doesn't truly appreciate the treasure she is. Jane might, but I'm pretty sure her younger sister has never valued Elissa in the way she should.

I place her bags down and wrap her in my arms, and for the next few minutes resume what we began down in the car below.

Finally, she breaks away with a laugh. "You'd better go, or else I'll never get inside."

"I'm a gentleman," I say. "I'm not leaving until I know you're safe."

"I'm tougher than I look."

"I know. But you're also important to me. So I'm not leaving until I know you're okay."

"So bossy," she mumbles.

"You know it."

Her lips curve to one side, then she winces. "Oh. I forgot. Matt and Lucy are still here."

"No, they're not. Matt messaged me earlier, as he had a meeting come up which meant they had to return earlier."

"So we're just facing my sisters."

"Be brave."

She laughs, pecks me on the lips then turns and opens the

door. "Don't come in," she says. "If you do, Lydia will have a thousand questions and you'll never get away."

I shift closer, draw her back into my arms. "I don't mind staying," I murmur, as my lips slide down her neck.

She laughs and pushes me away. "Go. Before either of us do something we regret."

"I'll call you in a little while, okay?"

"I'll be waiting." She smiles again. "Thanks again for a wonderful weekend."

"Thanks for coming. I loved getting to know you."

"And I loved getting to know you," she says.

A faint sound of, "Elissa?" makes me aware others want her.

"You should go," I murmur.

"You mean *you* should," she counters.

So I take the hint, blow her a kiss—thank God Georgia can't see me now—and retreat until her door closes.

Ten minutes later I'm back in my hotel suite, wondering how soon is too soon before I can call. I glance at the time. Order room service. Take a shower. Eat my just-delivered steak and salad wishing I was still with my dining companion from last night. Glance at the time again. My knee jerks as I wait. To heck with it. I grab my phone and call.

But she doesn't answer. I frown. Not to sound full of myself but I kind of thought she'd answer. Maybe she was having a shower or something. I don't want to imagine that—well, I do, but I shouldn't—so I leave a message instead. "Hey. Hope everything is okay. Call me when you get this, okay?"

I end the call, finish my now-cold food, and try to distract myself by looking over reports for tomorrow's meeting. My knee keeps jerking. Is there something wrong with me? Has this woman so quickly invaded my world that it feels incomplete without saying good night to her one more time?

I try again. I don't want to seem desperate, but I have a niggling feeling of concern.

This time she answers, "Liam!"

"Hey, how are—"

"Oh, Liam, I don't know what to do!"

"What's happened?" I've never heard that note of panic in her voice, panic that transmits to me and climbs up into my throat.

She's making a sniffly noise. Like maybe she's crying. Now I'm really worried. "Elissa?"

She exhales heavily. "It's Lydia. She's disappeared. We think she's gone with Wickley."

I close my eyes.

~

"I'M SORRY, ELISSA." Jane is still pacing around the apartment, twisting the ring on her finger. "I was having such a great time with Matt, I didn't keep track of what Lydia was up to."

Several thoughts run through my mind. Where was Lucy? Lydia is technically an adult, in Australia, anyway. When was she going to become responsible for her own actions? But Dad specifically asked we keep an eye on her. It's no use blaming Jane when Lydia's self-focused actions, done without thought for anyone else, are the reason she is missing. And with Gary Wickley. Although that hasn't been confirmed yet.

"What are we going to do?" I look up at Jane and realize she is waiting for me to reassure her. But honestly, I need reassurance myself. "When did you see her last?"

"Saturday afternoon. Matt and I were going to the Pioneer Square display, and Lydia didn't want to come, so Lucy said she would take her shopping."

"What about Saturday night?"

"Lydia sent a text around six o'clock to say she and Lucy were going to go out for dinner, and then they were going clubbing."

"Wasn't Matt worried about his sister?"

"He texted Lucy to find out more details. Lucy told him not to worry, that she would get Lydia home at a reasonable time."

"And did she? Did she get Lydia home at a reasonable time?"

Jane put her face in her hands and cried. "I don't know. Matt and I went driving to the Admiral Viewpoint Lookout and stayed way too long."

"How long?" I can feel my jaw clenching and teeth grinding.

"It was nearly dawn."

"Jane. You didn't—"

"No. Matt's not like that. We just talked and enjoyed the beautiful view. I didn't even realize how late it was until the sky began to show signs of dawn. Then we came back. We didn't want to disturb the others…"

"And you didn't notice Lydia wasn't here?"

"I slept late, and thought she'd come and gone again." The guilt in Jane's expression is killing me. It's not Jane's fault. I wasn't there either.

"But it gets worse, Elissa," Jane continues.

How could it be worse?

"The laws are different here. For Lydia to get into a club, she has to show ID."

"The same in Australia." I know Jane and Lydia have never lived in the city, and I'm not a clubbing, partying sort of girl, but I do know that it's illegal for people under eighteen to get into a night club, or to drink alcohol.

"The age limit here is twenty-one."

Twenty-one! Seriously?

"I didn't know the law, and Lucy didn't know that Lydia was only nineteen."

"Well, how did she get in?"

"Lucy thinks she got a fake ID from someone."

"Wickley."

"Oh, Elissa. Do you think so? Do you think he would do something like that?"

Before we can lament further, my phone pings.

"It's Liam. He's downstairs."

I go to the intercom and release the downstairs door lock to let him come up. We can't rush out anywhere until we make a plan. When I open the apartment door, Liam doesn't hesitate. Neither do I, going straight into his embrace and receiving courage from his strong arms. Then I remember Jane. She is watching with wide eyes as if she's stunned. I guess this elevation in our relationship is probably a surprise. But there's no time to examine that now.

"Come in." I lead Liam inside and he sits on the counter stool.

"We have no idea what to do." I switch the kettle on more from nervous tension than from any desire to make a cup of tea.

"I spoke to Matt Kennedy. He said that Lucy was really upset." Liam nods when I hold up the coffee jar in a silent question.

"Because?"

"Lydia met up with Gary Wickley at the club. Apparently, she'd been texting him the whole time. When Lucy suggested they better go home, Lydia ignored her and told her to go home."

"Poor Lucy. Lydia can be really nasty when she likes." Jane has put a herbal teabag in her cup ready for the boiling water.

"Did she find out where Lydia was going to go from there?"

"They didn't outline their plans, but Lucy had the impression they were going to go somewhere to stay overnight."

I feel a rocket launch in my stomach. Liam and I have gotten close over the last couple of days, but neither he nor I have pushed to get intimate. Not yet. I'm still holding out for a committed future, and if I understand Liam, so is he. But Lydia wouldn't be thinking about the future, commitment, consequences—any of it. She'd only be thinking about the thrill of the moment.

"Why don't you call her?" Liam suggests. "Ask her where she is."

Both Jane and I have tried numerous times, with no answer. I try again and get through to her vivaciously irreverent recorded voice message. I shake my head and see Jane shrink with disappointment.

"Who are you calling?" I watch as Liam scrolls through contacts.

"Gary."

"You have his number?" I feel surprised.

"He used to work for me, remember?"

I don't argue, despite the fact that I would have deleted him from my contacts list if he'd messed with one of my sisters.

Wait. He *is* messing with one of my sisters. Oh, this is too awful. What can we do? Both Jane and I stand by while Liam tries the number. There is more than an ounce of frustration in the way Liam hits the red end-call button.

"Where have they gone?" He spits the question out like an expletive.

All three of us are pacing like caged animals. The hot drinks are sitting untouched on the kitchen counter. I ask myself again, is this really my responsibility? Dad's voice pops into my head in an immediate response. *Look after your sister, Elissa.*

"What about friends location sharing. Do you have that?" Liam suddenly asks.

"I do, with Mum and Dad." It was easier to allow them access than have to answer phone calls every few hours asking where I was. I know Mum stalks me constantly, but at least she's happy, not worried about me being lost somewhere. "I don't have it with Lydia, but Mum might."

Jane picks up her phone. It looks as if she's pleased to have something positive to do at last. She calls Mum and puts the phone on speaker. It's probably an ungodly hour in the morning, but they might not have recovered from jetlag yet and still be on Washington time.

"What's the matter?" My mother is on high alert, the moment she picks up the call.

We briefly explain and ask her to check Lydia's location sharing, then—

"Why on earth is Lydia in Las Vegas, and why aren't you with her?"

The next half hour passes in a blur. Jane has elected to stay in the apartment in case Lydia comes back on her own, but Liam and I have gone to the private airfield, and he is logging in a flight plan. I can't help but smile at Jane's parting words.

"I thought you hated the private jet thing. Too pretentious."

"Not when I need to get to Vegas in a hurry."

"What about the carbon footprint?"

"It runs on fish and chips oil."

"What?" Jane's expression was comical, and in the midst of our stress, it was a small relief.

"I'm not kidding, Jane. Look it up. No carbon footprint to worry about here."

The thing is, I would probably have flown in the jet, fossil fuel or not, because I was anxious to find Lydia. She probably has no idea how her thoughtlessness is causing stress here and on the other side of the Pacific.

CHAPTER 13

I've never liked Las Vegas. I'm with my grandmother on that one. Flashy, trashy, with an underbelly of sleaze—there was a reason it was called Sin City. And that's only taking into consideration the huge greed that motivates so many here, not the other more seedy things that crawl beneath the glamorous veneer made famous in a hundred movies.

And there's something especially confronting when you arrive at an ungodly hour on a Sunday night—or is it Monday morning?—and still see people drunkenly wandering the streets, like they've lost their way.

We've hired a car and are slowly driving up the Strip, eyes scanning for any sign of Lydia. Elissa's mom has been sending us updates on Lydia's location, and I'm following as best I can, thankful that Elissa has a better sense of direction than most women I know. Between her and the GPS I feel like we might even have a hope.

I brake to avoid a group of young men as they stumble onto the road. One of them holds up a hand and grins like it's a joke they almost got run down. Another holds up a finger, and a third staggers to slap the hood of the Prius, and I feel a stab of alarm.

"Oh my gosh!" Elissa's voice holds fear, and I know I have to act calm.

The guy moves to the driver's door, as if to yell at me, and I stomp on the accelerator, and we leave him far behind.

"Oh, that was scary," she says, her voice wavering. "This place is nothing like in the movies."

We pass fake pyramids, castles, and the Eiffel Tower. We pass the Bellagio fountains, taking a final bow for the night in front of a reasonable crowd. We pass hustlers and tourists, all dressed far more reasonably for the milder temperatures than we are, dressed in Washington-warming jeans and sweaters. I do my best to keep my eyes on the road while scanning the sidewalk for any sign of Lydia and Wickley.

My grip tightens on the steering wheel again, as a hollow feeling, wholly unconnected to the lack of food, sweeps through my stomach again. This is my fault. I should've convinced Georgia to say something—to make a complaint to the police about Wickley, to press charges. The fact I haven't has gnawed at my conscience for months. I guess I always suspected something like this would happen again. But why Wickley has chased Lydia of all people I don't know.

"Why her?" I mutter.

I sense Elissa's glance, but I'm too busy watching the road. The traffic here is insane—stop-starts that mean we literally only move a few feet before the lights change again.

"I don't get it," she says. "It's not like we've got money."

Another thought pings. Wickley has proven he is predatory and opportunistic, seeking to exploit any potential that might advantage him. Could he somehow have become privy to my feelings about Elissa? It wasn't exactly a secret that I'd taken her back to the ranch with me. And I wouldn't put it past him to try to use Lydia to somehow get back at me. Heat ripples across my chest, and I white-knuckle the wheel.

"What does your mother say now?" I clear my throat to stop the growl. "Any updates?"

"Not yet." Elissa sighs. "I can't see Lydia wanting to visit a casino. It's not like she's ever got money to spare."

And she's underage. But it's entirely within Gary Wickley's character to get her a fake ID. Another charge of anger leaves me seething. "Try her phone again," I encourage.

Elissa presses redial—she's been calling this number all night —but sure enough, no answer.

"God help us," she whispers.

I find myself agreeing. The only way we will ever find them is with a miracle. This place is too huge, filled with lost souls desperate for more. Call me old-fashioned, but my grandfather's stories about the pitfalls of gambling always made me wary of trying my luck.

"What do people think—that a casino is set up as a charity?" he used to say. "Fools. Casinos are created to take your money. One thing those movies have right is that the house is designed to ultimately win."

I reach across and hold Elissa's hand, just as we hit the head of the traffic queue. Okay, this is it. Next green light and we're finally crossing.

Elissa's phone flashes. She snatches it up and holds it to her ear. I hear a squawk, then Elissa nods. "It's Mum. She says they're on Gass Avenue."

She punches that in to the GPS, and I scan the pixelating map, noting where I'll need to turn. The bright lights are starting to give me a headache, and I'm wondering if we wouldn't have been better off filing a missing persons' report, or hiring private detectives or security or something, but maybe we have a shot.

The light turns green and I accelerate, and we manage a whole block before we have to pause to turn left.

"Wait! She's now in Casino Center Boulevard."

"Did she say going north or south?"

"Mum?" Elissa tries to get an answer, but Mrs. Bennett's hysteria-laden voice is overwhelming. I had to ask Elissa to switch the phone off speaker—it's hard enough to concentrate on driving without Mrs. Bennett yelling in my ear—nothing she says is making any sense.

Still, the fact they're moving—or at least whoever has Lydia's phone is moving—suggests we're in with a chance of finding them.

The red-light changes, and I zip across, earning an angry horn blast and raised fist as I cut across traffic. I hope the police aren't watching.

Here the lights are a little less showy, but we're passing a wedding chapel, then another, which makes me think. Then swallow. *Dear God, no.* "You don't think she'd be at a wedding chapel, do you?"

"What? Don't be ridiculous. My sister might be hormone-crazy, but she's not about to do something like that."

"It's what Wickley did before."

"Oh." Elissa seems to wilt at the idea.

I really want to be wrong. I *really* want to be wrong. But I've been here before, well, not literally here, but a very similar scenario. My stomach is so tense I feel like I'll never have to do another plank or any other core-exercise again.

"Mum?" Elissa's talking on the phone again. "Anything new?"

I now have a choice. Turn left or right into Casino Center Boulevard. Which way should I go? I glance up the street, see an illuminated sign that announces another wedding chapel. Something inside jingles, just as Elissa says, "Turn right."

I obey and start searching for a parking space. The traffic here is much better, and I spy a space half a block away.

"She's stopped," Elissa says. "At the—"

"Red Rose Wedding Chapel?" I finish.

"Yes! Oh my goodness," she moans. "Lydia, are you insane?"

Apparently.

I manage to park, but before I switch off the engine, Elissa is slamming the door and running back to the chapel. It looks pretty hokey from outside, with a lit up arch, and white urns filled with what appear to be fake roses—red, of course. Tired faux-ironwork white chairs line the fence that separates an outside wedding area from the street, so you could elope in Vegas and have half the town walk by and wish you well. Classy.

I follow Elissa inside, brushing past a tired attendant at the front desk as I watch Elissa push open the door.

Then I hear a scream.

THE CHAOS that broke out in this poky little chapel might be considered comic, and if I wasn't so furious, I might have laughed.

"What are you doing here?" Lydia says in her high-pitched excitable voice following her scream. To be fair, she wasn't the only one who screamed. I gave a bit of a yell, the celebrant's partner yelped in fright and nearly fell off the organ seat, and—most pathetic of all—Gary Wickley let out a rather high-pitched expletive. It was in concert, but hardly in tune.

"What are *you* doing here?" I respond. "For heaven's sake, Lydia. Have you thought about what you're doing for more than a second and a half?"

"You're just jealous."

Oh my giddy aunt. I clench my teeth in frustration at the utter stupidity of it all.

"I apologize for the intrusion," Liam's deep voice overlays the rest of the hubbub. "Would you mind terribly if I have a word with the groom here? There are a few things he's not aware of."

The look on Gary's face is murderous. He really hates Liam, and that hate makes me lose any kindness I might have felt for him in the past. Not that I am feeling particularly kind at the moment.

The celebrant closes his book and signals for his partner to retreat, which they do behind a door at the back.

"What do you think you're doing?" I ask Lydia again.

She doesn't answer, but clings pathetically to Gary's arm, even as he begrudgingly follows Liam's signal to go outside with him. I grab hold of Lydia as she comes past.

"We need to talk."

Lydia rolls her eyes and lets go of Gary's arm as he disappears out the door.

"Why did you have to spoil our ceremony?"

I take a deep breath, but my patience, which has been running thin for a long time, finally gives out.

"Ceremony? Ceremony? Lydia, it is doubtful these weddings are legal in the first place."

"We don't need it to be legal. We just wanted to celebrate our love."

"Pfft! Don't be ridiculous. You've known Gary for, what, four weeks?"

"Hello, Miss Hypocrite, who's just flown down to Darcy's ranch. How is this different?"

"Because…it's different. I'm certainly not marrying someone I've known for a month," I snap. "Don't change the subject. You don't have a visa to stay in the country, you don't have any money to live on after your holiday money runs out, and Gary Wickley is a known predator when it comes to women."

Lydia casts a hurt glare in my direction. "How can you say that?"

"Because it's true. He has no interest in you."

"You don't know that."

"You can't stay in the US, Lydia."

"For your information, Gary has a brother-in-law who has money and influence, who will help us get set up here."

"Yeah? What's his brother-in-law's name?"

"Huh?"

"Who? What's the name of this brother-in-law?"

"I don't know. He just told me not to worry about things, that his brother-in-law would help us out."

Oh no. "He means Liam Darcy."

"What? No, he doesn't. He's not related to Liam Darcy."

"He's angling to be related to him. He's already tried it on with Georgia and abused her into the bargain."

Lydia opens her mouth to speak, but seems to come up short, but the frown on her forehead tells me she's beginning to put pieces together.

"Gary Wickley figures Liam will pay him money."

"Why would he?"

I just stare, hoping she will figure it out.

"Do you think Liam is serious about you?" Her tone is high-pitched again. "You hate him, don't you?"

"Keep up, Lydia. Why do you think I went to visit the ranch this weekend?"

She looks puzzled. Honestly, is she really that dumb, or is it she is so self-focused she hasn't paid any attention to what is going on with Jane and me?

"Do you really think Gary is trying to get at Liam's money?"

I screw my lips in a thoughtful pout. That is exactly what I think. Either that, or he is just trying to hurt Liam because he stopped the relationship with Georgia.

"I don't think you're right, Elissa." She crosses her arms. Any second now I'm expecting a little girl-like stamp of the foot. "I think you've completely misjudged him."

"Well, you can think that if you like, but I've been on the

phone to Mum and Dad, and they are literally freaking out. I'm not going to stand by and let you get into any sort of relationship that is likely to end up in abuse, nor am I going to let you get yourself embroiled in something that's going to prevent you from going home."

"What if I don't want to go home?"

"You'll have to talk to the immigration department if you want to sort that out. In a couple of weeks you will be here illegally, and if they catch you, they'll deport you, and goodness knows what trouble you might get into between now and then."

Lydia huffs and turns on her heel to march outside. I let out a sigh. I'm not her parent. She is technically an adult. Should I really even bother trying to keep her out of trouble?

The mild cool air is a relief in contrast to the heated intensity of the argument inside. I run into Lydia who is standing inside the picket fence looking up and down the street, her face a mask of worry.

"Where is he?" She turns on me. "You see? You've scared him off!"

I don't bother to point out that if Gary Wickley was aboveboard and a man of integrity, nothing would prevent him from standing by the woman he has proposed to marry. I check in the direction we parked the rental and see Liam coming back toward us, tall and confident. Where's Wickley?

"What did you say to him?" Lydia's voice is high-pitched as she runs toward Liam.

"Lydia." I walk quickly after her, hoping she doesn't go into one of her teenage tantrums. Please be a grown-up about this.

"You had no right to scare him off!"

Obviously, she's not thinking sensibly. I shouldn't have expected it. A girl who runs off to Vegas with a man she hardly knows is obviously not the epitome of sensible thinking.

"Where *is* he?" Poor Liam, having her scream in his face.

"Call him." Liam's voice is calm. "He can't be too far away. He's probably close enough to turn around and pick you up."

What is he saying? I throw him a wide-eyed glare, hoping it communicates my question.

Lydia gets out her phone and has punched in a number from recent calls. She holds it to her ear and begins to pace. "Pick up, pick up, pick up."

It's awful to watch. If Gary is like Liam suggests, he won't pick up.

"What did you say to him?" I've moved to stand next to Liam and use a low tone so that Lydia doesn't hear.

Liam just shakes his head.

"Does he care about her?" I probably already know the answer, but I'm beginning to feel my sister's pain.

"Once he found out there would be no money in it, he took off like a scalded cat."

Lydia throws her phone on the ground and cries out loud. "This is your fault!" She points her finger at Liam.

I go to her and take her in a hug. Her foolish heart is broken and it breaks me to see it.

CHAPTER 14

$\mathcal{W}$e're huddled in the ranch's big room, the fire roaring, the snow drifting outside a reminder of how we nearly didn't get to land this morning, thanks to the ice storm. Thank God for Marco, who got us down safely before the plane's wings froze. Thank God for Jackson, who met us and brought us back in time.

He must've thought us a strange lot. Elissa, Lydia, Marco, and myself. Marco, at least, managed to talk, but the rest of us have barely spoken since leaving Las Vegas several hours ago. I'm sure the Bennett sisters are as exhausted as I am, and not just from the midnight mercy mission, but from all the emotions involved as well.

And I bet no one feels as guilty as me. I'm the one who knew exactly what Wickley was capable of. I'm the one who could've done something but didn't. The only thing I felt sure to do was to beg Georgia to finally explain what happened, to which she's agreed. Perhaps she felt a little guilty too.

I've pushed back my meeting with the African water project investors, and Elissa has called Jane to set her mind at rest and sent her apologies so she's not going to college lectures today.

I'm not even sure if I'll make it back to Seattle this afternoon, but you gotta have a plan, right? And if this storm doesn't clear, well, I guess I can't feel too bad. And I know there are others who can step up for the project, and I might be able to Zoom in my appearance somehow. But I do know this conversation has to finally happen. Even if Georgia looks like she's about to throw up.

She glances at me, and I nod to offer reassurance. She knows that it's way past time this should be shared. She sighs, glances at the door as if to check Gran won't suddenly appear—she won't, I locked the door—then shifts on her seat.

"Lydia." My sister's voice is soft and calm. "I need to tell you something that happened to me. Something that happened with Gary Wickley." Georgia ducks her head, and I see her hands are shaking.

I gently massage her back.

Lydia still has a petulant look on her face, the stubbornness I know in her sister demonstrated in the crossed arms, tilted chin and glare.

Elissa is seated beside her and rubs Lydia's jeans-clad knee. "Listen to Georgia, Lydia. It's the least you can do."

Lydia's narrowed gaze and glance away suggest she doesn't agree.

Too bad, so sad. She needs to hear this anyway.

"I don't know how much you've been told about Gary Wickley," I say. "But he was employed here as one of the lead stablehands." We'd employed him to take care of the horses. Just hadn't figured he'd try to take care of Georgia too.

I glance at Georgia, but she seems to be struggling with what to say. I don't want to speak for her—I know she needs to own this, if Lydia is ever going to understand—but neither do I want her to have to go through the humiliation of explanations again.

Georgia's glance meets mine and I raise my brows at her. She bites her lip. Guess that's a no, then.

I continue, "I was often travelling for work, and wasn't always here, and I didn't know how close he was trying to get to Georgia."

Elissa is now also biting her lip, her hands clasped, her worried gaze shooting between me and my sister.

"He—" Georgia begins, then stops. She throws me a pleading look, but I nod, willing her to continue.

"He what?" Lydia demands sullenly.

"Apparently some women find him charming," I say carefully, when it's clear Georgia is not going to say anything more.

Elissa winces, and I have a terrible suspicion that maybe she found Wickley charming, once upon a time. I choose to not let that thought linger and lean forward, grasping GG's hand as if I can impart courage to her.

She sucks in air, and nods. "He...he was very nice to me when he worked here," she finally says. "He helped me with my horse, and we used to talk about all kinds of things. I, I wasn't used to men paying me attention—I went to an all-girls school, and when I'm home on the ranch I don't see too many people, anyway—so I found him exciting."

I can tell Lydia is paying closer attention now, even though she's looking at the floor. Her brow is creased, and her fingers have stopped twisting.

"We spent lots of time together, and got closer, and I thought he really liked me. I thought, I really thought he loved me."

Lydia stills.

"He tried to," Georgia's breath hitches, "he tried to get me to sleep with him," she finally admits. "Told me if I loved him I'd prove it. But I didn't want to. I knew Gran would have my hide if she ever found out I'd slept with someone she regarded as the stable boy."

I wince, conscious of the way Elissa is looking at me now, as if I'm responsible for my family's prejudice and pride.

"So when I refused, he kept pressuring me, saying he loved me. Finally he said we could get married, that then it'd be okay."

Her gaze lifts to connect with Lydia, who is staring at her, with wide blue eyes and a white face, and two spots of color high on her cheeks.

"What," Lydia licks her bottom lip nervously, "what happened?"

"He took me to Vegas. Said we could get married and nobody could stop us. I was old enough, and the ceremony there is legal. I was stupid enough to think he cared about me."

"What made you think he didn't care?" Lydia has fiery defensiveness in her eyes.

"I sent a text message to Liam, who was in Dallas for business." GG looks at me. "When Gary found out, he was furious. He called me all sorts of names I don't want to repeat. I thought he was going to hit me. I told him I was sorry, and then he turned all charming again." Georgia hangs her head and I know this is my cue to take over.

"When I got the text, I immediately flew to Nevada and found them just as they were about to sign the papers. I got them to sign different papers instead," I say grimly.

"What papers?" Elissa asks.

"Annulment papers," Georgia says. She sighs. "I was such an idiot. I really thought he cared." She seeks Lydia's eyes. "You should have heard the language he used when Liam came in. I really did think a fight would break out. It scared me."

It had scared me too. We'd stood toe to toe, with him yelling obscenities about me and Georgia, and I had seriously wanted to smash my fist into his mouth, but there were people standing around watching. Thank God they had been, otherwise I'm sure Wickley would've tried to sue me. That man would do anything to get his hands on our money.

"When I found out he only really wanted me for my money, I

felt so used and stupid." Her voice wavers, and I wrap an arm around her.

"He's a gambler," I say bluntly. "He's had gambling debts and I'm ashamed now to admit I paid them in order for him to leave Georgia alone. He was fired from his job here, but he never moved away from Trinity Lakes, and because we didn't want this getting out we never said anything."

"I was too embarrassed," GG admits, her hair falling across her face as she ducks her head.

Elissa moves to kneel before her, swiping Georgia's hair behind her ear tenderly. "You can't blame yourself," she says softly. "He sounds like he knew exactly what he was doing, preying on someone who was vulnerable."

Exactly what I'd said.

"I still do, though," Georgia admits. "I sometimes wonder if I'll ever be able to really trust a man again."

"Not all men are so manipulative," Elissa says, her glance sliding up to meet mine.

I study her, silently begging her to believe I'm not manipulative, when a stray thought steals in. What would happen if she ever found out I'd been investigating how to secure her placement on a research exchange?

I shake that thought aside. That's a question for tomorrow. There's still so much to do today.

"I...I didn't know," Lydia says, her gaze meeting mine for the briefest moment before she looks at Georgia again. "I thought he was a nice guy."

"That's what he likes to portray," I say.

My words echo around the room, the silence broken only by the crackle of flames.

"But I don't have any money." Lydia's frown deepens. "So maybe he *did* really like me. Maybe he still does."

"Honey, no," Elissa says, leaning back on her heels as she

pivots to face her sister. "I don't know why he targeted you, but it doesn't matter."

My chest grows tight. I'm aware of a reason why Gary might have thought it was worth pursuing Elissa's sister. Something to do with the fact I was pursuing Elissa.

"Remember he left you?" Elissa continues. "He hasn't replied to any of your messages yet, has he?"

Lydia tugs out her phone, her face falling when she sees it's true.

"You need to forget him," Elissa says gently.

"He's bad news," GG agrees.

I nod, willing her to believe us.

After a long moment, Lydia rubs her face, adding to the mess of makeup her earlier tears and tantrum have already impaired. Then nods.

And the relief I feel is akin to that on Elissa's face as she hugs her once-more crying sister, and I wrap my arms around mine.

I'M EMOTIONALLY EXHAUSTED. It's no wonder Dad has spent his life hiding in his books and reluctant to take on the storm that is Lydia. Probably the storm that is all of us—three daughters. I suppose I've had moments of emotional immaturity over the years, and rather than help us grow up, Mum has continued to stir the pot. More so with Lydia, the youngest and to my way of thinking, Mum's favorite. Still, this is not the time to be blaming Mum, or being overly self-righteous.

Watching Liam in the seat opposite me, I feel a wave of shame. The way I treated him early on has shades of Mum and Lydia. Time for me to be honest with myself. Seeing Lydia learn this lesson the hard way—seeing her heartbroken and humiliated—is not fun, but I'm glad she has the opportunity to do some soul-searching and hopefully think twice before jumping into something like this again.

Liam undoes his seat belt and shifts to the seat next to me. "What's running through your head?"

I shrug my shoulders. "I can't put my finger on it. That experience has worn me out."

He takes my hand and threads his fingers with mine. Warmth and comfort spread straight to my heart. Time to put the recent lessons into practice. Is this warm and fuzzy feeling that makes me want to curl into Liam's embrace and never move, love or some crazy mind-numbing infatuation?

I don't curl into his embrace, but I keep hold of his hand, and study the beautifully carved fingers and veins on the back of his hand. Love or infatuation? Where is this going? Can it go anywhere in any case? I'm here in the US on a limited visa and my time runs out in July.

"What are you thinking?" Liam speaks again, this time tilting his head close to mine in an intimate gesture.

"How did you figure Wickley knew about us?" This isn't what I'm thinking, but it pops to the front of my mind as a cover for the deeper, more confusing question that I'm afraid to ask.

"My ranch manager, Harry, told me he'd overheard some of the other workers talking. One of Gary's friends, who still works for me, was part of the conversation."

"What was being said?" I have a cold feeling in the pit of my stomach. Liam lets out a breath through his nose.

"They were kicking around some gossip."

I have turned and am staring at him with raised eyebrows. Will he tell me?

"I believe the words used were: 'The boss has a thing for that Australian girl.'"

I'm not sure how to take this.

"A thing?" The words pop out of my mouth. "What do they

mean by 'a thing'?"

"I've never shown any woman the attention I'm showing you."

I want to call him out about this: I might've Googled him—accidentally, of course—and learned about someone called Cassandra Bellingham, his last girlfriend. There were pics on Instagram that she could've only taken when on the ranch, followed by others—solo selfies—that scorched my eyeballs, and that I'm pretty sure would cause Liam's grandmother a heart attack.

But I don't say any of that. Because, from what Georgia has previously shared, Liam was well and truly over Cassie. Instead, my mouth decides to say, "So, not like Gary Wickley then?"

A pained look crosses his face.

"I'm sorry," I rush to say. "That was insensitive of me."

"I'm not toying with you, Elissa. I'm serious."

It's strange. Neither of us are smiling. The words are happy words—or they should be happy words, but there are a million different problems that keep clouding the future.

He leans in and kisses my temple. I'm draped in a wave of feeling. Love or infatuation? I'm wanting to vote for love, but Lydia's recent crazy actions have me considering infatuation. I am a Bennett after all.

I need to make a wise decision here. Liam is serious, and I can't lead him on if, come July, I hop on a Qantas flight and head back to Sydney, or Adelaide, or anywhere in Australia because I'm a citizen and can work there. I need to be honest with him. He said we could make it work, but I can't see how. Rushing off to Vegas for a hurried wedding is not going to cut it in the world of immigration and green cards. And is marriage what he means when he says he's serious? And am I ready for that as I'm just about to finish my masters in environment and sustainability?

"There's something brewing in your mind, I can feel it." Liam is studying my face.

I turn to him and force a weak smile. "I'm overwhelmed with what's happened the last couple of days. Is it okay if I just sit and ponder?"

He straightens in his seat, and I get the feeling I've offended him, though Liam doesn't strike me as the sort to take offense easily. But I'm not ready to take the lid off this particular can of worms yet. I'm still holding his hand, and I don't want to break that connection.

By the time we've landed in Seattle and taken a cab to my apartment, the mood is definitely morose. Lydia goes straight inside, and we follow. Jane is standing in the living area, a look of compassion on her face.

"Don't start, Jane." Lydia rushes past her and straight into her room.

Poor Jane. Her face always speaks for her, and she never gets a word out.

"I need to go. I've got a meeting." Liam's expression is begging for a response.

"I won't be a minute," I say to Jane. She's obviously dying to debrief, but Liam is first in my thoughts. I walk with him onto the landing and close the door.

"Can we have dinner, maybe tomorrow, before I fly back to Trinity Lakes?" The hope in Liam's eyes is obvious and my heart wrings. Love or infatuation? And if it's love, what can I do about it? Whatever it is, I need to make up my mind, because if it's only infatuation, I need to end it now before I destroy the poor man's heart.

"That would be lovely." I smile.

"Hopefully, we can talk some more after you've had a chance to rest."

"Yes." I lean into his outstretched arms and relish the warmth of his embrace. Love or infatuation? I really hope it's love.

CHAPTER 15

$\mathcal{R}$estlessness pulls at me, and I shift from the picture window overlooking the snow-covered hills and turn back to face my grandmother and sister. I'm feeling ganged up upon, the two of them sitting there watching me, while the questions that have been hurled in my direction dance around the room.

"Well?" Gran says.

She'd been horrified to see Lydia last weekend, my plan to keep the Bennett sisters out of her sight backfiring when they met in the hallway before we'd reached the garage.

Gran's gasp of dismay and obvious annoyance lessened when it became clear Lydia's exhibitionist nature had been well and truly put back in its box following Georgia's confession. But the sparks in her eyes shot in Elissa's direction had not diminished. Gran's barbed comments about Elissa only increased in this past week when business had forced me to cancel my dinner with Elissa and fly to New York instead. Fortunately, there'd been time to finish the presentation for the Africa project before my lawyer's call, but still. The past six days had felt like a never-ending crossing of the continent until I finally made it back here for Gran's birthday, something I'd never miss, even though I longed to be in Seattle. Especially after the question Gran has just asked me.

"I'm waiting," she says now.

I release a heavy breath, my gaze flicking to Georgia, who's now wearing a sly smile. I will say this: after last week's admission, GG seems a million times happier. Or maybe that's just the fact Elissa seems to have adopted her as another sister, or so GG has said, citing the daily text messages or phone calls Elissa has been sending. I hadn't expected that confession to bond them in such a way.

"William?"

My gaze snaps back to Gran. "Forgive me. My mind was wandering."

"My mind doesn't wander, and I'm nearly eighty-one."

"You tell him, Gran," Georgia says with a smirk for me. "I bet I know where his mind was wandering."

"Get your mind out of the gutter," Gran snaps.

"I'm not in the gutter," GG protests.

"And neither am I," I say. "I'm just thinking about how best to address this."

"What is there to address?" Gran demands. "I asked a simple question. Do you see a future with this girl or not?"

"With this woman," I correct, knowing that Elissa's feminist principles would hate being considered as anything less.

"Woman, girl, whatever you want to call her. Well?" Gran's eyes pierce me. "Do you see a future with this Elissa Bennett person?"

I push back my shoulders. "I do."

"Ooh, look! He's ready for a wedding with those words."

I shoot my sister a death glare. "It's way too soon for that."

"Is it?" she asks with mock-innocence. "I dare you to—"

"Oh, enough, Georgia!" Gran snaps. "They have barely known each other five minutes."

"But didn't you want him to find a wife?" GG asks Gran meekly.

I watch my grandmother's face as this sinks in, and the questions whirling through my brain settle into assurance. I didn't think I wanted a wife, but now, having met Elissa, I could definitely see a future with her. I *want* a future with her. I wasn't messing around. "I'm playing for keeps," I say aloud, the words ricocheting through my ears and heart and brain.

"You are?" GG asks, a big smile on her face.

I nod, and she jumps up and squeezes me. "Yes!"

"Georgia," our grandmother reproves. "I can't see how you think this is acceptable."

"But Elissa is *perfect* for him, Gran. You should hear her go on and on about environmental things. She's just as bad as Liam about it all. And she's funny, and fun, and Liam seems to think she's a good kisser—"

"Georgia." It's my turn to rebuke.

"What? It's not like it's a secret. You really *like* her, you want to *kiss* her," she says in a singsong manner I vaguely recall from a Sandra Bullock movie GG once forced me to watch.

Heat travels up my neck from the way Gran is looking at me. "I've been a gentleman, Gran." Haven't always wanted to be, but I've behaved.

"I would expect nothing less from my grandson," she says, adding an aristocratic-sounding sniff.

I exhale. "So?"

"So what are you going to do about it?" she asks.

"I thought you didn't like her," I state.

Maybe it's the honesty being flung around the room that makes her gaze falter, but I want her to see that she can't have it both ways.

"I know you want me to find a girlfriend and settle down," I say as kindly as I can. "But she's going to be *my* girlfriend, someone I lo-ike"—I quickly correct myself—"and want to spend my future with."

"You love her?" Georgia's eyes are round.

"I didn't say that."

"You didn't have to," she murmurs, looking at me with something that might be awe.

"Your feelings are that strong?" Gran asks.

I know a relationship isn't just about feelings, but takes commitment, too. And that's the thing. I'm willing to commit to Elissa, in whatever capacity that might look like. I nod. "I don't want to upset you, but I do think you should know I'm prepared to do whatever I can to convince her to stay."

"Hmm." She eyes me seriously. "I'll admit she takes some getting used to, but at least she seems to have more decorum than that other Cassie creature you brought home. She was not at all suitable."

"No, indeed," GG echoes, her smirk back again.

"But I cannot like that sister of hers," Gran says.

"Lydia is flying back with Jane today, is probably at the airport now, even as we speak. I think she'll be looking at this situation and thanking her lucky stars she got out of things as easily as she did." I chance a glance at Georgia, who offers a small nod.

"Elissa was telling me that Lydia is starting her university studies very soon," GG adds. Her eyes meet mine. "As will I."

Now it's my turn to grin. "You'll do amazingly well."

"Right?" GG grins. "I feel so much better about it all, and so much of that was due to Elissa." She turns to Gran. "That's what I mean. She helped me believe in myself again, took me to meet some of the creative arts faculty. She's really good-hearted, Gran. And I wouldn't mind if she was to hang around more permanently."

"But that's the thing," Gran says. "How can you see a future with her if she's going back to Australia one day?"

Now is the moment to admit it. So I do, wincing at how it sounds like I'm trying to manipulate Elissa's future. But it's not like she has to say yes to a research scholarship. She has options, at least. At least, more of an option than simply returning on her flight home.

"Wow." Georgia's eyes are huge. "What do you think she'll say when she finds out?"

"She's not going to find out," I say firmly. "The board knows that they're to keep my name out of it."

"Come on, Liam," she scoffs. "Elissa is smart. She'll figure it out."

I shrug. "Well, if she does, then I hope she knows I did it because I want her to stay."

"I don't think this is your wisest course of action, William," Gran says.

I lift my chin. "You wanted to know how I planned to have a future? This is how."

"I think you should find another way," GG says, her brow creased.

But it's too late. The deed is done. I could only hope if Elissa did find out she'd understand it was done with her best interests at heart.

I'M NOT AN OVERLY emotional person, but airports have this effect on me. My throat is swollen and my face muscles are quivering, even while I am working overtime to keep them still in the oh-so-calm position.

"It will only be six months until you come back home." Jane can read me like a book.

"You're lucky," Lydia says. "I wish I didn't have to go home so early."

I had hoped Lydia's thirst for fun and careless adventure might have been quenched following her tangle with Wickley.

"I'm going to miss you both." I hold my arms out for a group hug and they both respond. I can't help it. I begin to cry. They're my sisters. Lydia can drive me mad most days, but I love her. And Jane…what will I do without Jane?

"Cut it out, Elissa." Lydia pulls back. "You've got your luscious Mr. Darcy to keep you amused. Don't pretend you're dying to come home with us."

I'm not dying to go home, but I am feeling the separation from family, especially as we are lined up ready for my sisters to go through the security gate. I'm glad Mum and Dad went back to help Grandpa settle into a care home. When I've asked after Grandpa, Dad's told me he doesn't really know what's going on. I feel another surge of emotion at the loss of a grandfather. He's always been a cheerful supporter, like my father, and to know that he no longer understands who we are makes me sad.

"We'll video chat every week like usual." Jane squeezes me tighter. "And you do have Liam to keep you company." She pulls back and picks up her carry-on luggage.

I want to ask how things ended up with her and Matt Kennedy, but now is not the time. She'll let me know if there's anything for me to worry about.

They walk through the security, turning back every few steps to wave. The lump in my throat is nearly choking me, and my eyes are blinded by tears. Who knew I could be so attached to family?

Once they disappear from my view, I stand for just a few extra moments in case I get one more glimpse, then turn to travel back to my small apartment near the university. We gave up the holiday apartment this morning, after having packed and tidied. I had enjoyed living in a larger space for a while. Now it is back to the task at hand. My studies.

When I get inside, I see there are several envelopes on the

kitchen bench addressed to me. My housemate is out, which is just as well, because I'm feeling sad and depressed. As I flick through the pile, I see one that looks interesting.

It's written on university letterhead and is from a research department, one that specializes in environment and sustainability.

Dear Ms. Bennett,

Our faculty are pleased to offer you a research scholarship in environmental studies, due to start at the end of the academic year. It would be of great benefit to our department, and we hope you will be able to accept. We are offering the place several months early to give you time to apply for the appropriate visa, which, we understand, you will need to further your stay in the United States.

Please advise us as to your interest in this research position as soon as possible.

Sincerely,

Etc

A research scholarship? Two thoughts run through my mind. How did they know? And why me?

Without thinking twice, I unpack my laptop and power it up. I want to know more about this research project, and why the head decided that I should be chosen for a scholarship. At least this gives me something to occupy my mind and dispel the sadness that drifted home with me.

Why don't you call Liam?

Where did that voice come from? My slightly confused heart seems to be clambering for attention. I desperately want to call Liam, but I still haven't found a way that our relationship can work. Except ...

I pick up the letter again. The scholarship is for a year. If I can get the appropriate study visa, that means it's eighteen months from now until I'll have to go back home. While that is wonderful, it still has an end date. I want to stay with Liam forever. I want to know he truly cares. That he might one day love me. I think about his Gran's challenge for him to find a wife and mother for his children. When I first heard about it I'd cringed. Now I'm almost ready to fill an application for that position. Would eighteen months be enough time for us to know if our relationship was a good and permanent thing?

I pick up my phone and punch in the number for the university department who is offering the scholarship.

"Ah, hello. Could I speak to... Professor Darling, please?"

"May I ask who is calling?" a very officious voice on the phone asks.

"My name is Elissa Bennett, and I've just been offered a scholarship on a new research project in your department."

"Yes. That's right."

"Could I speak to Professor Darling?"

"He's not in at the moment. What is it you would like to know?"

Now that she's asked the question, I'm not sure what to say.

"Ms. Bennett?"

I clear my throat. "Um. Yes. Ah. I'm somewhat surprised to have been offered the place."

"I believe the scholarship was created especially."

"Especially? By whom?"

"A philanthropist company, goes under the name of Pemberley Sustainable Research."

A rock drops to the bottom of my stomach. Liam.

"Is there anything else I can help you with?"

"Ah, no. Thank you."

"I'll tell Professor Darling you called. I daresay you will want to arrange a meeting with him soon if you plan to accept the offer."

"Yes. I daresay."

I end the call in a daze. Liam has arranged a research scholarship and somehow got them to offer it to me. What the—?

My first thought is to run and find him and hug him until it hurts.

This is followed closely by my second thought: Did I win the scholarship because the university has noticed my work, and believes I'm the best person for it, or because my boyfriend has thrown money at it?

My third thought: Who cares? I get to stay in Seattle and work in the area that is my passion, AND I get to see Liam as often as I want.

Then the last thought, which was the one that ended my last meditation on where Liam and I will end up: it's only eighteen months. I don't want to build a deep relationship with the man and then have to wave him goodbye as I walk through the international security gate, bound for Australia.

Why couldn't he have offered me the wife and mother of his children position? That is so much more permanent.

Because you've only known him five weeks, idiot.

But sometimes, five weeks is all you need.

Now I'm sounding like Lydia, except there is no way on earth I would agree to get married in a tacky Vegas chapel. It's the full church, bridesmaids, pink swans and ice sculptures for me or nothing.

Where has my head gone? Pink swans indeed. As if. I'd settle for white.

But marriage... to Liam. He hasn't even mentioned anything of the sort—other than his grandmother's dare. I'd better back it up a bit. At this stage, he has surreptitiously bought me an extra twelve months in the States. Perhaps I'd better talk to him and see if he's got anything to say about it, or if he's hoping I won't notice.

CHAPTER 16

So, this isn't exactly what I'd envisaged for Valentine's Day. I was imagining something a little more romantic than the ranch's dining room but given the past week of missed phone calls and interruptions to those few conversations we actually had, I've determined that the best plan involved kidnapping Elissa for the weekend. Well, plus a few extra days when work intruded once again.

But Gran has seen I've improved, that the reason I check my phone so often isn't because of work, but because of Elissa. She makes me smile like no-one else can. Whether it's her sass or sly tease or sharp mind I feel...lighter around her. More myself. That she gets me. And that the world has possibilities. Endlessly good possibilities. Especially if she says yes to that research scholarship she's been 'awarded.'

My guts churn, as the women continue making conversation. Elissa hasn't mentioned anything about the scholarship yet. I wonder if she will. Unease ripples through me when I think she might learn it's from the Foundation. But surely she'd see that just means I want—I need—to have her near?

Gran is now talking about roses, and I listen, surprised to

learn Elissa knows a few things about flowers as well. But then, this woman keeps surprising me with all the things she knows, her interests as varied as mine can be. I'm pretty sure she's impressed Gran in these past few days.

One benefit of being stuck in the office for most of Sunday was that it did give Gran a chance to get to know Elissa. Of course, Georgia was already deputy head cheerleader of the Elissa fan brigade—after me, of course—but Gran's approval of my 'friend,' as she liked to call Elissa, has always been a little tenuous.

Apparently the women visited one of the churches in Trinity Lakes that Gran likes to attend sometimes, then spent the afternoon cooking. When I finally emerged from meetings concerning a last-minute hitch to the Burundi project it was to a heavenly scent, something that drew me, moth-to-flame-like, to the kitchen, where I discovered Elissa with floured hands instructing Georgia to pull a tray from the oven, while my grandmother looked on with something that looked like approval in her eyes.

"Oh, William, you are finally finished?" Gran had said, turning to me. "Come here and taste these scones. Have you ever tasted anything quite so delicious?"

Before I can take another step, Georgia has shoved a small plate with an already buttered scone at me. "Did you make this?" I ask Elissa.

Duh. It's obvious she's the chef. But I never picked her as the domestic type.

"Go on, tell us what you think," GG says.

I take a bite—of course I'm going to say it's nice, because otherwise you might as well call this relationship dead and buried—and the still-warm buttery goodness slides down my throat. "This is amazing!" I manage past spluttered crumbs.

Gran looks at me, but I don't care about etiquette. "It tastes a little sweeter than what I'm used to."

Elissa smiles, and we have a brief guessing game about the mystery ingredient until I am forced to admit I don't know what it is.

"It's pumpkin."

"Really?"

"That's why it looks a little more orange than normal," GG helpfully points out.

I ignore her, and move toward Elissa, who is wearing an apron that looks like one I remember Mom used to wear. "I think I like you wearing an apron."

She rolls her eyes, but I can see a smile threatening to poke out as she backs away. "You like your women domesticated."

"Pretty sure Elissa is already house-trained," GG offers.

My grin grows as even Gran manages a girlish-sounding giggle. Now that's a sound I haven't heard in years.

"But not too house-trained," Elissa says, now backed up against the white farmhouse sink. She can't go any further. But I can.

I swoop in and kiss her, and she freezes for a moment— probably because we have an audience—then she relaxes and places her hands around my neck.

Then I hear laughter.

Oh. I pull back, study her with my brows raised. "Did you just put flour on my back?"

"On your neck, actually."

"And your hair," Georgia adds, which seems to prove an invitation for Elissa to rub her hands in my hair, as I threaten to tickle her.

That was two days ago, and I'm relieved that the stiffness of Saturday morning's flight, when something seemed to have been bothering her, has now relaxed into fun and ease that has continued. Gran has even gone so far as to tell me she thinks my mother would've liked Elissa, that they share a passion for making the world a better place, while still caring for family.

"She makes you smile, dear boy," Gran said, patting my cheek. "And I'm prepared to overlook many things if she can make you look at ease."

But I never dreamed that my grandmother's hard-won approval would extend to her insisting on joining us for our first Valentine's Day meal.

Elissa's gaze now lifts to meet mine, her smile peeking out as if she, like me, doesn't know what to do with the game of twenty questions that's currently being played. This was so not what I imagined when I'd asked Elissa to pack that red dress from weeks ago.

"And I want to know about your grandfather," Gran asks now, as if she hasn't had a chance to ask that any time in the past four days. "Have you heard anything more about how he's doing?"

"He's slowly adjusting to the home," Elissa says, stroking the gold-etched rim of her plate. "Dad says Grandpa has his own room, with a view out to the gardens and birds, so that's something he enjoys looking at."

I catch Georgia sneak a lifted-brow look at Gran, then look back at me. They're up to something, but what, I don't know. "Did you have something to do?" I ask Georgia. "Maybe somewhere else to be?"

She snickers. "Why? Aren't you enjoying my company?"

I narrow my gaze at her. Honestly, sisters can be annoying sometimes. She's lucky I love her.

"Did you have something to say?" she asks sweetly, with a less-than-subtle tilt of her head at Elissa. "I dare you to say it, Liam."

I don't need her dares for me to say what needs to be said. I glance across the table at my guest. Elissa is hiding her own smile behind her hand, her wide eyes taking it all in.

"I do," I say. "And much as I love your company," I say this to

Gran, "I'd find it easier to talk to my girlfriend if you weren't here."

Georgia sighs and stands. "I can take a hint."

"About time," I mutter.

"I too, know when I am not needed," Gran says. But there is no suggestion of miffed feelings. Her smile at Elissa suggests that it's simply tease.

Finally they leave, and I can exhale. But Elissa is still sitting too far away for my liking. I pick up my plate and flatware and move to situate myself next to her. "I'm starting to wish I'd never brought you here."

"Excuse me?"

"I didn't realize I'd have to fight my Gran and sister in order to talk to you."

"Your life is *so* hard."

"You know it." I pick up her hand and kiss it. "Thanks for coming again."

"I'm glad for the chance to do so. To be honest, it's been a little lonely in Seattle with my sisters gone."

"Family is important, isn't it?"

She nods, her gaze fusing with mine.

I see there are questions there still, but I ignore them, taking my time to kiss her. I barely notice as the door opens.

"Mr. Darcy."

I reluctantly pull away as Brenda comes in with a tray and two silver-domed plates. She places these on the table, checks we don't need top-ups of our drinks, then moves to the door. "Enjoy your night."

"Thanks, Brenda. Appreciate you staying later too."

She smiles, and nods, and I'm left with a funny feeling that maybe she's been drinking the same funny juice as the women in my family. They all have the same look about them.

The next few minutes pass as we ooh and ahh over our meals. Brenda has really outdone herself tonight. And to be honest, she cooks better than any establishment in Trinity Lakes, so why would I want to serve Elissa something inferior? Not when I can finally have this private moment with her.

"I'm sorry today hasn't exactly been the romantic Valentine's Day I'd imagined."

Elissa gives a small shrug, her focus on cutting her food. "I've never really celebrated it too much, so I had no expectations."

"What? You mean you weren't expecting a flight to Paris?"

"Nope."

"No ten-course meal?"

"I love steak," she says, popping in a mouthful.

"No enormous bouquets of red roses?"

"I prefer roses that smell nice."

I think she actually means it. That's another quality that has impressed my grandmother. Elissa Bennett says what she means, is compassionate and not self-seeking, and is certainly not a gold-digger.

"Honestly, Liam, I've really enjoyed being here," she says, resting her knife and fork on the edge of her plate. "I really don't need anything more."

"Not even the little something I got you?"

She smiles. "That might depend on what that little something is."

It's a bracelet with diamonds on it. Something classic, classy, and Gran-approved. It's burning a hole in my jacket pocket. Now to wait for the perfect moment to give it to her.

"Still, I sure didn't mean to have my work interrupt our time so much."

"Please. As if I need to have you entertain me when the lives and livelihoods of people are at risk. How is the water project going?"

Discussing the water needs of Burundi sure makes for romantic conversation. But the way she's asking questions suggests she's actually interested, which only makes my heart warm even more to her.

"I think it's so awesome what you're doing." Her eyes light. "I'm so impressed that you do what you do."

"Maybe you should come see it with me," I hear my mouth saying. Whoa. Did I really just say that out loud?

She blinks. "Really?"

"I plan to go in a few months, and if you were interested we could find a way to make that happen."

"I'd love to, but…" She bites her bottom lip, and I can see that thing that was bothering her a few days ago is back.

"But what?"

"But something has happened," she says slowly.

I know a prickle of fear. This doesn't sound good. The rest of the food on my plate is growing cold, but I don't care. What we're about to discuss is important. "Care to elaborate?"

Her gaze connects with mine. "Do you know anything about a scholarship I've been offered?"

I swallow. Glance at her. Wish for a distraction, anything. "Uh…"

There's a light knock, then the door opens. It's Brenda again. "Excuse me, sir, but I was wondering if you're ready for dessert."

"That sounds great," I rush to say. "You like dessert, don't you, Elissa?"

"My mum always likes to say life is short so eat dessert first." She eyes the food still on my plate and her eyebrows hitch a little. "She also said no dessert until you eat all your vegetables."

I hesitate to point out the contradictory nature of those two statements, settling for, "It's a good thing she's not here then, isn't it?"

"On so many levels," she agrees.

Brenda's smile is twitching and she collects our plates, promising to return in a moment. Which leaves me with this moment of figuring out how to explain.

"Well, Mr. Darcy?" Elissa says now.

"You know, you look very beautiful tonight," I say.

"Don't change the subject."

"Can't you take a compliment?"

"I can, but your timing suggests you're trying to distract me."

I smile, lean in, and brush a kiss along her cheek and down her jaw, which elicits her giggle and a sigh. "I promise I'm not trying to distract you. I just—"

The door swings open again and Brenda has returned, holding a platter and two bowls. I straighten and try to not look like I'd gotten into dessert already. I'd given her instructions about the main, but only indicated I thought Elissa would appreciate something sweet for dessert, so I left it up to her.

But then I see what's written on the chocolate mousse, and as my mouth dries, I know exactly why Georgia and Gran had looked so smug earlier. Delicately inscribed in white chocolate amid crafted candy roses is a phrase I've never said to a woman. Not to a girlfriend at least. Because until now I've never wanted to say that to a woman.

It's like Georgia has stolen the secret of my heart and written it for us all to see.

I love you.

I LOVE YOU? My heart stops for a moment and then thuds back to life. It's right there in sugar frosting, but how does that translate into words? I search Liam's face, where color has climbed in his cheeks. He is still staring at the pudding like it has shocked him.

"Is this Georgia's handiwork?"

"What?" He looks at me with what looks like a shade of horror.

I tilt my head in the direction of the elaborate artwork.

It looks like Liam's mouth has gone dry as his Adam's apple struggles to swallow. I need to hear this from him in actual soundwaves and decibels, because I suspect this is his sister's attempt to hurry things along, and while I love the sentiment...

"Elissa—" He picks up my hand and his gaze homes in on mine.

"Yes?" I can feel my eyebrows have almost reached their upper limit.

"Technically speaking..."

Just say it, Liam. Or don't. You're killing me here.

"I didn't know about these sentiments." He waved his hand in the mousse's direction, and my heart falls along with my face.

"However," he tilts my chin up, "they reflect my heart to perfection."

I am staring him straight in the eye. I have to as he's holding my face. But I don't want to look away. I want to see sincerity in his soul. And I do.

"Do you think you could say it out loud?" I'm being pushy, but I'm funny like that. Inferred endearments are one thing, but blatant expression is so much better.

"I...love...you." His tone sounded like a question, as if he was worried I might react and throw the dessert in his face.

"I love you too." His face breaks into a warm grin and he moves from holding my face to kissing it—enthusiastically, leaving no patch of skin unattended.

Phew. "That was awesome. Let's do it again." I smile at him, but his attention is diverted. Again. I watch as he pulls out a velvet covered jewelry box. It's long, so I know it's not a ring. Am I glad about that, or disappointed? No time to examine those thoughts as Liam has opened it and is holding out a diamond bracelet.

"Oh, Liam. This is gorgeous." And expensive. It has white and pink diamonds, and while I love it, I feel the clash of my ideals fighting with my emotions.

"Don't you like it?" He sounds unsure, and I realize he can read me better than Jane.

"I love it. Really, I do. And I will treasure it forever."

"But?"

"You know I'm not the sort of girl who needs expensive jewelry and clothes and stuff. Not when I know there are so many people in the world who have so little to live on."

Liam kisses me again, then pulls back and begins to fasten the bracelet on my wrist. "That is one of the reasons I love you, Elissa. That you think more about other people than you do yourself."

I can feel the weight of the diamonds on my wrist, and I turn it around to inspect it closely. "This is beautiful. Thank you."

"But I must remember not to do it too often?"

"You must remember not to do it at all again. I will treasure this, but I will also treasure a gift of helping humanity whenever possible."

"Your wish is my command." He sits back and is looking satisfied. "Just so I'm clear, this means no luxury vacation?"

"Burundi, perhaps."

"Done, though I can guarantee there won't be much luxury involved in that trip. And no more jewelry?" He has a smug look on his face.

I shake my head.

"Not even a ring?"

The words hit my stomach and cause a whoosh of antic-ipation.

"All right. You drive a hard bargain. We can talk about a ring —one day, in the future—if that's what you really want."

"Good." He turns around and puts his bowl of dessert in front of him and picks up the spoon.

"So about this scholarship—nice try for distraction, by the way." I mean to get to the bottom of it. He puts his spoon down and I can see guilt in his expression.

"Are you mad at me?" He has those large puppy-dog eyes, dismantling any opposition I might have had.

"What, for setting up a bogus scholarship for me?"

"It's not bogus. I believe in the program."

"I confess I was a little mad. At first."

"Why?"

"Because I feel a little funny knowing I haven't earned the position."

"Trust me. You've earned it. Your head of faculty was singing your praises."

"Yes, well, look who he was singing them to. You don't think that your position as major benefactor might not have colored his opinion?"

"I don't believe so. I believe he thinks you are outstanding in your field of current research."

It was nice to hear this praise second hand, and I feel warm with gratitude. I pick up my bowl of dessert from the tray as well, and we stop talking while spooning in the deliciously creamy chocolate mousse.

"There's just one more thing." I put my spoon down in my empty bowl.

"Anything for you, my love."

"It is another eighteen months when the scholarship will finish, and if I can't get a new visa, it will run out. What will happen then?" I wave my hand back and forth between us.

"That's when step two will take place."

"Step two?"

He gives me a wink and a huge grin lights up his gorgeous face. I can only imagine, but it seems good, whatever it is.

"What's step one?" I ask.

"Something like this." Liam leans in again, takes my face in his hands, and I easily engage in the deepest, most loving and soul stirring kiss.

The sound of laughter and clapping intrude into my cloud of

passion, and I pull back. The joyous noise is coming over the intercom. Georgia, Gran, and Brenda are whistling and hooting.

I search Liam's eyes. He's smiling, despite the fact we obviously have an audience. "You forgot to turn the security cameras off in the dining room, didn't you?"

THE END

~

CONTINUE the Trinity Lakes adventure in

Meredith Resce's *The Ocean Between Us* and
Carolyn Miller's *Love Somebody Like You*

~

Sign up for Carolyn's newsletter here
(& get a free book!) here: https://www.
carolynmillerauthor.com/connect

Sign up for Meredith's newsletter here:
http://www.meredithresce.com/contact-meredith/

A NOTE FROM THE AUTHORS

Thank you for reading *Daring Mr Darcy* - we hope it made you smile! As avid Austen fans we enjoyed the challenge of bringing *Pride and Prejudice* into modern times for a rom-com audience, and hope you enjoy the nods to Austen's beloved classic. (In case you're wondering, Carolyn wrote Liam's perspective, and Meredith wrote Elissa's)

This book is set in Trinity Lakes, a contemporary romance series set in a fictional part of east Washington state, based on such beautiful towns as Chelan and Walla Walla.

Enjoyed this taste of Trinity Lakes? Then make sure you continue the Trinity Lakes adventure in

Meredith Resce's *The Ocean Between Us*
and
Carolyn Miller's *Love Somebody Like You*

Reviews help other readers find new-to-them authors, so if you can spare a moment to write a quick review at Goodreads / your place of purchase, we'd be very grateful.

ABOUT CAROLYN MILLER

Carolyn Miller lives in the beautiful Southern Highlands of New South Wales, Australia, with her husband and four children. Carolyn loves travel, movies, music and food (which necessitates a love for exercise!), and has worked as a high school English and Learning and Support teacher.

A long-time lover of romance, especially that of Jane Austen, Georgette Heyer and LM Montgomery, Carolyn holds a BA in English Literature, and loves drawing readers into fictional worlds that show the truth of God's grace in our lives. Her contemporary romance series includes the Muskoka Shores small town romance series, the Original Six hockey romance series, and the Independence Islands series. Her historical series include the Regency Brides and Regency Wallflowers series. Find out more about her books (& sign up to get a free book) at www.carolynmillerauthor.com

ABOUT MEREDITH RESCE

South Australian Author, **Meredith Resce**, has been writing since 1991, and has had books in the Australian market since 1997.

Following the Australian success of her *Heart of Green Valley* series, they were released in the UK.

The Ocean Between us is Meredith's 24th published title.

Apart from writing, Meredith teaches high school students. She is an avid reader, particularly Christian fiction. She is a fan of British costume-drama television series, and British cosy mystery shows. Jane Austen, L.M. Montgomery and Charles Dickens are favorite classic authors. Meredith is a country-girl at heart, and takes every opportunity to visit the farm where she grew-up.

Aussie rules football and cricket are her choice when following televised sport. Come on Aussies!

Meredith often speaks to groups on issues relevant to relationships and emotional and spiritual growth.

Meredith has also been co-writer and co-producer in the 2007 feature film production, *Twin Rivers* now available on Amazon Prime.

With her husband, Nick, Meredith has worked in Christian ministry since 1983.

Meredith and Nick have three adult children. Find out more about her books at www.meredithresce.com

ALSO BY CAROLYN MILLER

Refining Josie

Historical:

<u>Regency Wallflowers</u>
Dusk's Darkest Shores
Midnight's Budding Morrow
Dawn's Untrodden Green

<u>Regency Brides: Legacy of Grace</u>
The Elusive Miss Ellison
The Captivating Lady Charlotte
The Dishonorable Miss DeLancey

<u>Regency Brides: Promise of Hope</u>
Winning Miss Winthrop
Miss Serena's Secret
The Making of Mrs Hale

<u>Regency Brides: Daughters of Aynsley</u>
A Hero for Miss Hatherleigh
Underestimating Miss Cecilia
Misleading Miss Verity

'Heaven and Nature Sing' from the Joy to the World Christmas
novella collection

ALSO BY MEREDITH RESCE

Trinity Lakes series
The Ocean Between Us

License to Meddle series
Organised Backup
In Want of a Wife
All Arranged

Historical Drama / Romance
The Manse (The Heart of Green Valley series #1)
Green Valley (The Heart of Green Valley series #2)
Echoes in the Valley (The Heart of Green Valley series #6)
Mellington Hall
Cora Villa

Time Travel Adventure
For All Time

Made in United States
Troutdale, OR
09/20/2024

22981343R00119